"We're Close Friends, Daniel. That's All We Are."

"Yeah, well, maybe that's what we thought, but obviously we were mistaken."

She shook her head fiercely. "No. I've never been more certain about my feelings where a man is concerned. You're a good friend, Daniel, and I don't want to mess that up. The two of us have been getting along just fine for two years with things between us at the friendly stage."

Speak for yourself, Daniel thought. He'd been a nervous wreck for the past two years, watching Olivia come and go from a distance, being a part of her life only on the fringe. *Friends* was the last thing he wanted to be with her.

Dear Reader,

There's so much in store for you this month from Silhouette Desire! First, don't miss *Cowboys Don't Cry* by Anne McAllister. Not only is this a *Man of the Month*— it's also the first book in her CODE OF THE WEST series. Look for the next two books in this series later in the year.

Another terrific miniseries, FROM HERE TO MATERNITY by Elizabeth Bevarly, also begins, with *A Dad Like Daniel*. These delightful stories about the joys of unexpected parenthood continue in April and June!

For those of you who like a touch of the otherworldly, take a look at Judith McWilliams's *Anything's Possible!* And the month is completed by Carol Devine's *A Man of the Land*, Audra Adams's *His Brother's Wife*, and *Truth or Dare* by Caroline Cross.

Next month, we celebrate the 75th *Man of the Month* with a very special Desire title, *That Burke Man* by Diana Palmer. It's part of her LONG, TALL TEXANS series, and I know you won't want to miss it!

Happy reading!

Lucia Macro
Senior Editor

Please address questions and book requests to:
Silhouette Reader Service
U.S.: 3010 Walden Ave., P.O. Box 1325, Buffalo, NY 14269
Canadian: P.O. Box 609, Fort Erie, Ont. L2A 5X3

ELIZABETH BEVARLY
A DAD LIKE DANIEL

SILHOUETTE *Desire*®
Published by Silhouette Books
America's Publisher of Contemporary Romance

SILHOUETTE BOOKS

ISBN 0-373-05908-6

A DAD LIKE DANIEL

Copyright © 1995 by Elizabeth Bevarly

This edition published by arrangement with Harlequin Enterprises B.V.

® and TM are trademarks of Harlequin Enterprises B.V., used under
license. Trademarks indicated with ® are registered in the United States
Patent and Trademark Office, the Canadian Trade Marks Office and in
other countries.

Printed in U.S.A.

ELIZABETH BEVARLY

is an honors graduate of the University of Louisville and achieved her dream of writing full-time before she even turned thirty! At heart, she is also an avid voyager who once helped navigate a friend's thirty-five-foot sailboat across the Bermuda Triangle. "I really love to travel," says this self-avowed beach bum. "To me, it's the best education a person can give to herself." Her dream is to one day have her own sailboat, a beautifully renovated older-model forty-two-footer, and to enjoy the freedom and tranquillity seafaring can bring. Elizabeth likes to think she has a lot in common with the characters she creates, people who know life and love go hand in hand. And she has the inside track on maternity—Elizabeth and her husband recently, and joyously, welcomed their first child, a baby boy.

For Jade Louise Bevarly,
the first of the next generation.
Welcome to the world, kiddo.

Prologue

"He looks just like you, Livy."

"Oh, Sylvie, he's only ten hours old. How can you say he looks like anybody?"

Olivia Venner stood, in her nightgown and robe, between her sister, Sylvie, and her best friend, Zoey, staring through the glass into the hospital nursery and wondering what on earth she'd gotten herself into. She knew she wasn't the first single mother to appear in the world, and certainly she wouldn't be the last. But for the past nine months, she'd focused so much of her energy on simply getting Simon born that she had neglected to fully consider everything the blessed event would bring afterward. Now, as she studied the tiny baby wrapped in a pink-and-blue-striped blanket, with a blue knit cap warming his bald little scalp, she could only shake her head in wonder.

He was hers, she thought, and no one else's. She alone was responsible for his upbringing—his needs, his wants, his education, his morals, his values. The task facing her was a daunting one to say the least. And she was just now beginning to feel the impact of all that was to come.

"He does kind of look like you, Livy," Zoey said, splaying open over the glass perfectly manicured fingers tipped in fire-engine red. "Look at that little upturned nose, and those dimples. His eyes are pretty dark—they'll more than likely turn brown like yours. And he'll probably have dark hair... once he gets hair, that is. Both you and Steve have brown hair."

"Oh, Zoey, you and I have seen millions of babies in our line of work. You know how quickly they change. They never look like anything but a squalling, puckered blob when they're born. Simon could wind up being just like his father."

"God forbid," Sylvie said, not quite under her breath.

And not without Olivia hearing the remark. "Look, I know Steve turned out to be kind of a jerk—"

"Just like every other guy you've ever dated," her sister filled in unnecessarily.

Olivia continued without commenting. "But the fact remains that he is Simon's father."

Zoey emitted a rude sound. "Oh, and he's really illustrated how important that fact is to him, hasn't he? What was it again he did the minute you told him you were pregnant?"

Olivia sighed hopelessly, wishing she could forget about that night. "He refused to believe the baby was his, then he got on his motorcycle and rode straight out of town."

"Without even telling you where he was going," Sylvie interjected.

"And without even saying goodbye," Zoey concluded.

Olivia stared first at one woman and then the other. Her little sister resembled her not at all with her scrubbed, gee-whiz face, spiky blond haircut and wide blue eyes. Sylvie generally threw people for a loop, because she looked like an idealistic high school cheerleader but in fact worked in one of Philadelphia's poshest restaurants as a bartender. She could go toe-to-toe with any sailor, truck driver or construction worker who dared look at her askance, and generally left her opponent whimpering.

Zoey, on the other hand, looked like exactly what she was in her starched blue hospital scrubs, with her fiery red tresses woven into a tight French braid—a no-nonsense, height of efficiency, to-the-point neonatal nurse. She and Olivia had met in nursing school, and the two of them had worked here in the maternity ward of Seton General Hospital, one of south Jersey's oldest and most esteemed hospitals, since graduation nine years ago. Olivia herself held a position in the obstetrics unit. The two of them had been friends long enough for Olivia to know how dedicated the other woman was to her profession, and long enough for her to realize that Zoey, too, was as faithful a friend as her sister, Sylvie, was.

Together, the two women had been Olivia's support system throughout her pregnancy. She couldn't have made it without them. Now, however, they were beginning to get on her nerves.

"Look, I'll admit Steve wound up being a far cry from Mr. Right," she conceded, "but for a while there, he and I had something really special."

Sylvie twisted her mouth in disgust. "*You* had something special, Livy. Steve didn't have a clue."

"In spite of that, I feel like Simon's going to be cheated by not having a man around," Olivia said softly. "And frankly, I'm not sure what I'm going to do without one around, either."

"You'll be better off, that's what," Zoey replied without hesitation. "You're going to be a great mom, Livy. But Steve as a father... That's something that totally violates every rule of nature."

"But a child should have a father," Olivia insisted. "Especially a little boy. Simon's going to need a man in his life to emulate and look up to, someone solid and decent and loving."

"Well, that pretty much leaves out all the guys you generally go for," Sylvie said.

None of the women, including Olivia, denied the truth in the statement. Instead, all three continued to gaze through the glass at the little bundle of flannel and pink flesh that was her son.

"Hey, what about Daniel?" Sylvie said suddenly.

"Daniel?" Olivia asked.

"Daniel McGuane, your neighbor," Sylvie clarified with a speculative little smile. "You know, the boy next door?"

Olivia made a face at her sister. "I know which Daniel you're talking about. I just don't understand why you're mentioning him."

"He'd be a great father figure," Sylvie pointed out. "He's smart and gentle and nice, very upstanding and a fine figure of a man. He's got a steady job working with his hands and all that. He's the salt of the earth. And he's right next door. How convenient."

Before Olivia could say more, Zoey added her own plug. "And not only would he be a great father figure, he'd be a great stud muffin, too."

Olivia's mouth dropped open in disbelief. "Are we talking about the same Daniel?" she asked. "Daniel McGuane? My next-door neighbor? A stud muffin?" She almost choked on the last two words. Really, it was too funny to imagine.

Sylvie nodded. "He's yummy."

Olivia looked to Zoey for confirmation.

The other woman vigorously nodded her agreement. "Very yummy."

Olivia thought about it for a moment, but shook her head quickly. "No, not Daniel. He's too... too... too *nice* to be a stud muffin. I mean, he's the nineties answer to Wally Cleaver, for Pete's sake."

"I think he's yummy," Sylvie said.

"Me, too," Zoey echoed with another nod.

Olivia sighed in mock disgust, forgot about her next-door neighbor and turned to look at her new son again. Ten hours ago, he had been dragged howling into the world against his wishes, naked and fragile and completely unprepared for what life would cast before him. He was just a baby, she thought as she felt tears welling up in her eyes. And she was just one woman. How was she going to help him learn to live and love all by herself? How could she alone do the job normally assigned to two parents when she had never even been responsible for a pet? How on earth had she managed to assume such a phenomenal task by herself?

What was a mother to do?

One

The wind howled around Daniel McGuane's house, snatching at the shutters and catching hold of the back door, whisking it open before slamming it closed again. The lights flickered once, twice, three times, then extinguished themselves completely. In the darkness, he felt his way to the kitchen and fumbled for the drawer containing a flashlight, then flicked the switch to the On position. Nothing. He shook the flashlight vigorously and tried again. But another empty click of the switch left him remaining in darkness.

"Dammit," he swore under his breath.

As he stumbled toward the gas stove, he banged his knee against one of the plastic-backed chairs at the table and swore more colorfully than before. Finally he managed to locate a box of matches, and he struck the head of one with his thumbnail. In the limited circle of light that surrounded him, he worked quickly, searching frantically through two more drawers for extra batteries. His eyes had just lit on an unopened package when the flame of the match seared his fingertips. Instinctively, he dropped it to the floor, then quickly stamped it out with his foot. Working awkwardly in the darkness, he replaced the flashlight's old batteries with new and finally afforded himself a weak ray of light.

Outside, the rain picked up speed and the thunder roared more ferociously. He wondered if Olivia was all right next door.

She'd just brought the baby home from the hospital a few weeks ago. If his power was out, no doubt hers was, too. Was that safe? he wondered. Didn't babies need all kinds of newfangled electrical-type stuff to keep them running properly? And didn't they have to be recharged occasionally? The electrical-type stuff, he amended quickly, not the babies, of course. Although now that he thought about it...

Daniel sighed and ran a big hand restlessly through his pale, sandy-colored hair. He knew as much about babies as he did about biochemical research, he thought morosely. And seeing as how he made his living as a carpenter, that wasn't much. Still, this was turning into a pretty major storm. Olivia might need something.

"Oh, hell, who am I kidding?" he asked no one in particular. Olivia Venner might need many things, but one of them most certainly was *not* Daniel McGuane. She'd made that more than clear on more than one occasion.

When Daniel had been in the market for a new house two years ago, a Realtor had brought him around to show him the one he now inhabited in Collingswood, and he'd bought it on the spot. Not because it was everything he'd been looking for—quite the contrary, in fact—but because Olivia Venner and two of her friends had been lying on lounge chairs in her backyard next door. They had been listening to loud Tito Puente music, sipping margaritas and wearing the smallest bikinis he had ever seen. One brunette, one blonde, one redhead. For just the briefest of moments, he was certain he had been sacked by a bus earlier in the afternoon and had entered some fabulous, beer-commercial afterlife.

But when Olivia had turned her head to find him ogling her and her friends, she'd lifted her drink in salute and said, "Hi, I'm Olivia. Welcome to the neighborhood." And Daniel had smiled, knowing what he was seeing was wonderfully, erotically real.

He couldn't quite remember all that had happened after that. He recalled blathering out his name idiotically and trying to squelch all the sexual fantasies that had burst to life in his feverish brain. Then he'd stumbled back into the house and asked the Realtor where to sign.

Only on moving day had he realized what he'd gotten himself into. Not only had he discovered that Olivia Venner was already involved with someone else, but his new house had seemed to be on its last legs. Fortunately, he was a carpenter. Unfortunately, he couldn't afford to pay himself for his own full-time labor. So two years later, he was still working on his house. And working and working and working.

The neighborhood itself was in an older, more tranquil section of southern New Jersey, and that much at least met with his approval. He'd been hoping for a little peace and quiet after the raucous, party-hearty apartment complex he'd moved into after leaving home sixteen years ago. Back then, he'd considered the phrase "bachelor living" to mean hard-drinking, roughhousing, staying out until dawn and dating dozens of women at any given moment without attaching himself to any one in particular.

But over the years, his ideas about life had gradually altered. And two years ago, he'd decided he wanted a change from the wild times. With an inheritance from his father, he'd begun his search for the perfect house—nothing fancy, nothing large, but something with the potential to become a family-type dwelling. He didn't quite know why he wanted a family-type dwelling when he didn't have a family, but as he'd begun work on his new home, he'd decided the old place did indeed have potential. Slowly, but surely, it was coming along.

However, he still had quite a way to go, he thought now as he trained the beam of the flashlight over the two sawhorses and tarpaulin that furnished his dining room. Quite a *long* way to go. He sighed.

A smack of thunder boomed above him, and he jumped, certain the roof was falling in. The wind gusted fiercely, scraping the branches of a colossal oak tree in the front yard along the length of the house outside. The sound made him think of the claws of a huge monster raking themselves around the building, and he shivered. He supposed that, even as an adult, one never did quite escape the childhood fears that storms this violent seemed to rouse.

Olivia and the baby must be frightened out of their wits, he thought. Maybe he'd just run over and check to make sure everything was okay.

He threw a battered foul-weather jacket on over his jeans and white T-shirt, but didn't bother with any other protection. He was only going next door, after all, he reminded himself as he tucked the flashlight into his jacket pocket and exited through the back door. And the trees surrounding the two houses were broad and thick with late-spring leaves. Hell, he probably wouldn't even get wet. Turning up the collar of his jacket, he began the sprint toward the house next door.

Simon flexed his little fingers and made a contented sound as he suckled at Olivia's breast, oblivious to the storm raging outside. Her lights had gone out just as she was lifting him from his bassinet, so she'd collected the four candles from the china cabinet in the dining room and lit them on the end table beside the couch. Now as she sat cross-legged with her plaid flannel shirt unbuttoned and Simon fastened to her breast, the golden candlelight reflected in wisps of amber off the downy dark fuzz on the baby's head. Olivia smiled. He was indeed going to have dark hair. If he ever did grow hair.

The house was oddly quiet in spite of the rain, wind and thunder, so she hummed softly to the baby as he fed, a disjointed, meaningless tune she made up as she went along. His eyes met hers in the candle glow, and for just a moment, Olivia forgot about how terrified she was of raising Simon alone. For this brief time, she could give him everything he needed. He was hungry, he needed nourishment, love and care, and at least she had all of those things to give him.

"Olivia!"

She started at the sound of Daniel's voice coming from outside her back door. Her neighbor's sudden introduction into such an intimate moment with her son caught her off guard, but she was surprised to discover she didn't resent the interruption. When she turned to call out that the door was open and that Daniel should come on in, Simon's mouth fell away from her breast and he began to fret. Immediately, Olivia shifted him to her other breast, then resumed their earlier position, tucking him securely onto a throw pillow beneath her arm and supporting his head with her hand. It occurred to her again that such placement was more reminiscent of a quarterback carrying a football than of a mother cradling her child, but it seemed to work best for feeding him.

From behind, she heard the back door thrown open on a gust of wind, followed by the stamp of heavy boots before the door was slammed shut again.

"Olivia!" Daniel called out more loudly. "Are you all right?"

"I'm in here," she said calmly, skimming the backs of her fingers along Simon's cheek in an effort to soothe him. He did not appreciate the loud noises her neighbor inflicted upon what had been a completely peaceful scene only moments ago. "Shh," she whispered to the baby. "Shh, it's all right." She began to hum again, this time choosing an old lullaby that never failed to quiet him.

As Daniel's heavy steps drew nearer, she tugged the right side of her shirt over her bared breast, but continued to nurse the baby. She felt no stirring of modesty or inhibition, simply because the activity she was sharing with her child demanded neither reaction.

"Hello, Daniel," she said when she felt him standing behind her. "What brings you out into a storm like this?"

When he didn't answer right away, she looked up over her shoulder to find him staring down at the baby suckling hungrily at her breast. There was no more than thirty feet of yard separating their houses that he'd been forced to cross, but he was soaking wet from the rain. Water dripped from the damp, dark blond hair falling over his forehead, spiking his lashes and making them seem longer somehow. His pale blue eyes appeared even lighter than usual in the soft glow of the candles, the odd illumination darkening the hollow jaws beneath his sharp cheekbones.

She couldn't possibly think of Daniel McGuane as yummy, she assured herself, recalling the way Sylvie and Zoey had described him. He was too handsome, too healthy, too well-bred-looking, too perfectly formed. He claimed none of the roguish imperfections or dangerous qualities she preferred in a man. Still, she supposed he wasn't bad. Kind of attractive even, really, in a wholesome, boyish, clean-cut sort of way, if that was what turned you on. Which of course, where she was concerned anyway, it did not.

"I, uh...uh, I-I'm sorry," he stammered, his gaze still fixed on the baby at her breast. "I didn't realize you were... I mean I thought you might be... Oh, hell." She saw him blush before he spun around and concluded simply, "I'm sorry. I didn't mean to intrude. I was afraid you might be over here...you know...needing something. I wanted to be sure you and the baby were all right."

Olivia grinned at his thoughtfulness and what was an unmistakable discomfort at witnessing such a scene. "It's all right," she assured him. "I'm just feeding Simon. You're not intruding. Have a seat."

She could tell he was reluctant to do so, but he seemed equally unwilling to leave her alone while the storm raged outside.

"Come on," she encouraged him. "Get out of that wet coat and hang it over one of the kitchen chairs. Simon will be finished soon, and I'll put him down and fix you a cup of tea to warm you up."

Daniel moved—or more correctly, bolted, she thought with a smile—away from the sofa, and she heard him shrug out of his jacket and do as she'd instructed him. When he returned, he sat down in an overstuffed chair opposite the sofa, letting his gaze travel over everything in the living room except her.

"When the power went out," he began quietly, "I wasn't sure if you'd be okay over here. I was afraid something might go wrong. I wasn't sure if the baby would be okay without electricity."

Olivia smiled, unable to keep herself from teasing him. "Oh, no. Simon's fine. He's one of those new babies you can get now that runs on rechargeable batteries. You don't have to plug him in at all."

"Very funny," Daniel said wryly without looking over.

She chuckled. "Babies have been around a lot longer than electrical outlets have," she reminded him.

"That's true."

A long silence followed until Olivia said softly, "Thanks, though, for checking up on us."

Her quietly uttered thank-you was a balm to Daniel's frazzled nerves. He had been prepared to come over and find the baby screaming in terror at the lightning and thunder, and Olivia half out of her mind with worry and a few fears of her own. Instead he had intruded on what was probably the most serene-filled moment he had ever witnessed. He should have known better. Olivia Venner had always been able to take care of herself, as much as he hated to admit it.

He stared at an oil painting of flowers that hung over the fireplace, but what he saw instead was a tiny baby sipping thirstily from Olivia's full, round breast, and her fingers softly caressing the infant's cheek. She was humming again, he realized in some distant part of his mind. A lullaby. As he continued to look blindly at the painting on the wall, he remembered the first time he'd seen Olivia in her teeny bikini, recalled all the times he'd seen her leave for work in her crisp white nurse's uniform. He saw her wearing cutoffs and a cropped black T-shirt, perched on the back of a huge Harley-Davidson hog behind that jerk, Steve.

Then he turned his attention to the woman seated at the center of a circle of light across the room. Her soft brown curls tumbled unrestrained around her face, a face made fuller by the weight she had gained during pregnancy and she now still carried. She was more rounded everywhere because of that, he noted, her body seeming more lush now, more womanly as a result. Funny that he hadn't much paid attention to that before, he thought. When Simon pushed himself away from her breast, she lifted him against her shoulder and began to gently pat his back. Her eyes met Daniel's then, and she smiled.

And in that moment, something Daniel had always suspected but had never quite allowed himself to believe became utterly clear in his mind. He was in love with Olivia Venner. And he had no idea what he was supposed to do about it.

The baby made a tiny, hiccuping sound then, and she laughed softly before wiping his mouth with the corner of the cotton diaper draped over her shoulder. She rubbed her hand in small circles over Simon's back, and he hiccuped again. This time Daniel laughed along with her.

"I guess he's finished with supper," he said.

She nodded. "In about five minutes, he'll be fast asleep."

He watched mother and child for some moments in silence, then asked, "How have you been, Livy?"

Olivia's heart did a funny little dance at the sound of her nickname coming from Daniel's lips. He didn't usually call her that. "I've been okay," she told him.

Although she had meant to say more, for some reason she couldn't form the words. So she simply continued to rub Simon's back in silence, but couldn't quite prevent herself from staring past the baby and into the eyes of her next-door neighbor.

"Really?" he asked her. "I haven't seen a lot of you lately. For the past couple of months, it's just been in passing. I've thought about you a lot. Wondered if you were all right. If everything was okay with the baby. If Steve—"

"Steve's out of the picture," she said succinctly.

Daniel's eyebrows arched at that. She wasn't sure if he was surprised, skeptical or sorry. His only comment was a cryptic "Oh?"

She felt Simon's head nod against her shoulder. He was valiantly trying to ward off sleep, so she shifted him into a more horizontal position. Now that he was finished eating, she was more acutely aware of her unbuttoned blouse and wished she had a third hand to close it. Although she was pretty well covered, she couldn't help but notice when she looked down that the soft swell of one breast seemed more prominent than normal thanks to the shadows thrown by the flickering candlelight.

When she glanced up at Daniel, she noted that he seemed to be noticing, too. An odd thrill of electricity shot through her at the realization of his unmistakably sexual awareness of her, but she tamped it down. Her hormones were still in an uproar after giving birth, she reminded herself. That was the only reason for her reaction. That and the fact that she'd been too long without any intimate contact with the opposite sex. The last thing she wanted right now was a roll in the hay. Just thinking about the act was painful.

"So where's Steve now?" Daniel asked, and she suddenly remembered they had been having a conversation.

She tried to sound careless as she replied, "I have no idea."

"Doesn't he know about the baby?"

"He knows."

"Oh."

She could see that Daniel was about to pursue the topic further, so she rose from the sofa, silently thanking Simon for having the decency to fall asleep when she needed him to so that she could excuse herself for a few moments to put him in his crib. She balanced the baby in one hand and a sputtering candle in the other as she headed upstairs and tucked him in, switching the infant monitor to battery power so she'd be able to hear him downstairs when he awoke again. He roused a little when she started to move away, then gurgled anxiously.

"What?" Olivia asked him quietly as she bent over the crib again. "What's the matter, sweetie? It's okay. Mommy's right here. And Daniel's downstairs, too. You'll be all right."

Simon's eyes widened a bit at the mention of Daniel's name, and she laughed. "What?" she continued in the breathless whisper people tended to adopt when addressing infants. "Do you like Daniel McGuane? But you just met him. Yes, you did—you just met him. You're as bad as Aunt Sylvie and Aunt Zoey. Next thing you know, you'll be telling me Daniel's a yummy stud muffin, too." She chuckled when Simon's mouth opened in a big yawn.

"Well, I'm not gonna fall for it," she told her son with a laugh and a soft chuck under his chin. "No, I'm not. No, I'm not. You can all talk until you're blue in the face, but Daniel McGuane just isn't mommy's type." She bent to nuzzle the baby's nose with her own. "No, he isn't. No, he isn't. He may have nice blue eyes and a sweet smile, but Mommy's just not interested—no."

Simon's eyes fluttered closed again, and she stood over him for several more minutes until she knew he was asleep. After she tiptoed out of the nursery, she passed by her own bedroom to don a brassiere and rebutton her shirt. Almost as an afterthought, she quickly ran a brush through her unruly hair.

Boy, she was a mess, she thought when she caught a glimpse of herself in the mirror. The humidity had turned her hair into an unmanageable mop of curls, and the only nonmaternity clothes that fit now were a couple of pairs of sweatpants and a few man-size shirts Steve had left behind. If Daniel McGuane could throw a lascivious glance her way, he must be one of the loneliest men alive.

When she descended the stairs to the living room, he was gone. She found him in the kitchen, standing at the gas stove as he waited for the water in the teakettle to boil. His flashlight was on, upended to throw a wide circle of light on the ceiling above him. That's when Olivia noticed the other baby monitor sitting on the kitchen table, realized the switch was positioned at On and noted that it, too, had been changed over to battery power. She closed her eyes and prayed that Daniel had been elsewhere when she and Simon were having their little heart-to-heart. She held her breath as she waited for him to say something.

Then he turned and fixed her with an intent gaze. "Where do you keep your tea bags?" he asked.

She expelled the breath as steadily as she could. "In that Humpty-Dumpty tin over the kitchen window. It's herbal tea, I'm afraid. My doc says no caffeine for me while I'm nursing. But I think I still have some of the regular stuff in a cabinet."

She went to the cabinet in question just as Daniel was turning away from the window. They bumped into each other, front to front, and for a moment neither seemed able or willing to move away. Olivia had instinctively lifted a hand to his chest on impact, and now registered vaguely the presence of warm, solid muscles beneath the damp fabric of his shirt. She had seen the weight-lifting equipment in his basement dozens of times, and she supposed it had occurred to her that he worked out regularly, but she'd never really given it much thought. Yet faced with the evidence of the results, she had no choice but to think about Daniel McGuane sitting shirtless and sweaty, muscles bulging as he pumped iron.

"Uh, sorry," she mumbled as she stepped away from him, trying to banish the graphic image burning itself into her brain. "I, uh...the regular tea is over there." She pointed over his shoulder. "Behind you."

"That's okay," he said, his voice seeming rougher than she'd heard it before. "I'll have what you're having. I try to stay away from caffeine myself."

Of course, she already knew that about him, she remembered. Daniel McGuane didn't drink, didn't smoke, ate strictly in compliance with the food pyramid recommended by nutritionists, got plenty of exercise, took very good care of himself and lived a quiet, stable life. Those were some of the things she had always hated about him, she reminded herself. Not that she was such a wild woman herself, but she had been known to travel down the path of unrighteousness once or twice in the past, and she certainly succumbed to the temptations of sugar and caffeine and an occasional beer or glass of wine. Daniel just seemed to be so together, so in control of his life, where she often felt as if she were about to become unraveled. And she supposed, in some ways, she resented him for that.

"Right," she said softly. "I knew that."

"So did you get Simon settled in all right?"

Her head snapped up at his question, but Daniel was busy unfurling tea bags and placing them in mugs. He didn't seem to have meant anything by it. "Yeah, no problem," she muttered as she rubbed her hand unconsciously, trying to dispel the lingering sensation of touching him.

Her gaze traveled to the infant monitor again, and she bit her lip anxiously. Oh, who cared if Daniel had heard the things she'd said to her son? Olivia thought. She hadn't been lying. Daniel McGuane wasn't her type. And despite the assurances of Sylvie and Zoey that the man in question was

a total stud muffin who would be the perfect role model for
her son, she just wasn't interested.

Still, she thought as she took in his broad back and solid
forearms, noting the wet tresses clinging to his neck, maybe
Simon would like him.

Two

Later that night found Daniel lying on his living room sofa, staring into the blackness above him, waiting for his lights to come back on and thinking about Olivia Venner. Outside, the rain and thunder had come to an end, but the wind still rattled the house viciously. He had stayed with Olivia and Simon until the worst of the storm had passed, telling himself it was only because he wanted to make sure they were all right, but knowing it was in fact simply because he wanted to be with Olivia.

He still couldn't quite dispel from his mind the image of her seated on her sofa in the candlelight, feeding her son. Her house, like his, was close to seventy years old, the flowered wallpaper and aged furnishings looking almost as if they'd been there since the place was built. A homemade, multicolored afghan was thrown casually over the back of the couch. And amid it all, Olivia had looked like the consummate mother, bonding with her child in a way Daniel himself would never be able to comprehend. It was a side of her he'd never witnessed before, one so domestic it shouldn't have roused him sexually. But it had. Fiercely. Completely. Indomitably.

He turned to his side and recalled for perhaps the hundredth time how her voice had sounded coming over the infant monitor in the kitchen after he had absently switched it over to battery power because of the storm.

Daniel McGuane just isn't Mommy's type. No, he isn't. No, he isn't... Mommy's just not interested—no....

The statements didn't hurt him quite as badly now as they had the first time he'd heard them. But he still hurt. If Daniel had needed confirmation that Olivia didn't care for him as anything other than a friend—which, of course, he hadn't—he now knew for sure that he was somewhere below Sylvie and Zoey on her list of people she'd most like to be with.

He rolled to his back again. Hell, now that Simon had entered the picture, he'd probably be below Mister Rogers and Bert and Ernie, too, not to mention that damned purple dinosaur with the goofy laugh.

When he first heard the loud *crack* outside the house, Daniel didn't much respond, thinking it was just the thunder starting up again. But when it was followed by a long, louder *creak*, he sat up, startled. And when that was followed by a sonorous *crash*, he jumped up and sped for the back door. Throwing it open, he looked up to see that a thick limb comprising a good one-quarter of the biggest of the oak trees surrounding his house—the one between his own dwelling and Olivia's—had snapped free. Worse, than that, though, it was resting on what had once been Olivia's back porch but was now a pile of broken wood, glass and plaster.

"Livy!" he cried as he bolted out the door in his bare feet. He covered the short distance between the two houses in seconds, heading for her front door, which he threw open without knocking. Vaguely, he made a mental note to take her to task again for not locking herself in properly, then called her name out in a panic one more time.

"I'm in here," she called out from her kitchen, her voice sounding thin and weak. Simon's squalling came from the same direction, and for one bleak moment, Daniel was certain he would find them both hurt.

Oh, God, he thought as he sprinted toward the sound of the crying baby. Had they been in there when the branch had come falling down? Were they trapped beneath it? Injured? Dying?

When he catapulted through the kitchen door, he saw Olivia standing on the opposite side of the room, cradling a still-wailing Simon against her shoulder. Even in the dim light provided by the candles, he could see that her dark eyes were huge and frightened.

"Are you all right?" he asked, barely able to control the fear that still choked him.

She nodded quickly. "I was fixing some hot chocolate when I heard this loud popping sound. I looked up, and the next thing I knew, there was this unbelievable crash, and the glass in the back door exploded when a tree branch came through."

"Simon?" Daniel asked, the single word all he could manage when he realized what could have happened if she had been standing four feet farther to the left of the stove.

Olivia nodded again. "He's okay. Just scared."

"And you're okay?" he asked again, still not convinced.

"I'm fine, Daniel. I'm just scared, too. Everything happened so fast."

He looked up at the ceiling. There was probably no danger of any further collapse. Olivia's house was almost identical to his own in layout, so he knew the back porch wasn't a major support feature. Still, there was no way to be certain yet just how much damage the tree limb had done for sure.

"You and Simon are staying at my place tonight," he stated without preamble.

Olivia's gaze followed his own. The ceiling looked fine to her. And she could put some cardboard over the back door to keep out the rain. She opened her mouth to tell Daniel that although he was nice to offer, there was absolutely no reason for her to spend the night at his house. Then she remembered the baby in her arms. If it had been her alone she needed to worry about, she would have had no trouble insisting that Daniel was overreacting and that she would be just fine in her own house. But she wasn't willing to risk even the slightest chance of danger where Simon was concerned. Funny, she thought, how quickly a baby changed things.

"All right," she said. "Let me just pack up a few things that we'll need."

Daniel nodded, surprised that she had agreed to his command so quickly. He had intentionally adopted his best nononsense-don't-argue-with-me voice when he'd insisted she stay at his house, but he honestly hadn't thought such an affectation would sway her. Olivia was simply a woman who wouldn't be told what to do. Yet this time she had given in without a single argument.

Simon, Daniel recalled immediately. She hadn't acquiesced because he had demanded she do so, but because she feared for the baby's safety, if not her own. Oh, well. At least he could rest easy knowing she would be all right at his place until he could deduce the damage done to her house. Of course, he himself would be anything but all right now, knowing Olivia was sleeping so close by.

He sighed. Would there ever be a time in his life, he wondered, when what Olivia Venner was doing wouldn't matter to him at all?

Olivia awoke slowly the following morning, not quite certain where she was. When she had fallen asleep the night before, the wind had been howling, Simon had been fretting, and she had been lying in Daniel McGuane's bed. And Daniel, of course, she remembered now, had retired to the

couch downstairs. Today there was no sign of yesterday's
tumultuous weather. The early-morning sunlight sifted
through the half drawn miniblinds, throwing bright, horizontal stripes across the floor and bed. A purple finch sang
happily somewhere outside, and the baby cooed content-
edly from his bassinet in the corner of the room.

She sat up, shoved a handful of dark curls out of her eyes,
and suddenly realized she and Simon weren't alone. Daniel
sat holding Simon in the rocking chair he had insisted on
bringing with them last night, his head bent down over the
infant as he murmured meaningless sounds to soothe him.
Olivia straightened the scooped neck of her flowered,
sleeveless nightgown and swung her bare legs over the side
of the bed.

"Good morning," she said, her voice quiet and rusty
from sleep.

Daniel glanced up with a slight smile, then quickly back
down at the baby, then up again in an unmistakable—and
undeniably heated—double-take. Olivia was suddenly and
acutely aware of her state of dishabille, and she reached
quickly for her robe. It wasn't like Daniel hadn't seen her in
her nightgown before, she tried to remind herself. On more
than one morning, she had greeted him while wearing such
a garment on those occasions when he left for work while
she was on the back porch watering her plants. Then again,
she supposed awakening in a man's house—or, more specifically, in a man's bed—constituted a scenario that was a
bit more intimate than a passing hello.

"Good morning," he replied in return, his blue eyes soft
in the half light of the bedroom. "I'm sorry—I know I
shouldn't be in here, but I was passing by and heard the
baby."

Olivia smiled at him. "Why shouldn't you be in here?"
she asked. "It's your room after all. You apologize too
much, Daniel."

He shrugged, then looked down at the baby curling a
loose fist around his finger once again. "But you deserve a

little privacy. It's just that you were still asleep and I thought I'd try to keep Simon occupied for as long as possible so that you could get your rest." His eyes met hers again as he added, "No offense, but you've been looking pretty tired lately, Livy."

He'd done it again, she noticed. He'd addressed her by the nickname that only those closest to her normally used. Any other time, she'd take offense if a man called her something reserved for family members and especially close friends. She hadn't even liked it when Steve called her Livy. But coming from Daniel, the name sounded and felt oddly natural, as if he had more right than anyone to use such a term.

"No offense taken," she assured him. "I *am* pretty tired lately. Newborn babies tend to take a lot out of you."

Daniel was about to reply that he could imagine, but stopped himself. The fact of the matter was, he couldn't begin to imagine what it must be like to generate a new life within one's own body. The realization that Olivia had done just that still frankly amazed him. He noted again the lush curves of her body that were a result of Simon's arrival. Her white terry-cloth robe hung open, and the neckline of her gown skimmed low over the swells of her breasts. She was a nursing mother, for God's sake, he tried to remind himself. So why couldn't he stop thinking about what it would be like to make love to her?

He forced the thought away and said, "If I can do anything to help with Simon, you just have to ask. I mean, I don't know a lot about babies. . . ." He glanced down at the infant in his arms again. "Actually, I don't know the first thing about babies, but if you need me . . . for anything . . . I'm here."

Olivia smiled. "Thanks, Daniel."

Another thought struck him then. "How long do you have off before you have to go back to work?"

"About eleven more weeks. I'm taking full advantage of the Family Leave Act." She rose from the bed and stretched, lifting her arms well above her head. The action brought the hem of her short nightgown dangerously high on her thighs, and Daniel sucked in an involuntary gasp he hoped she didn't hear. But she continued blithely, "I was granted twelve weeks of maternity leave from the hospital—unpaid, naturally—and I requested my regular two weeks' vacation on top of it."

"What—" he began, stopping to clear his throat when his voice seemed to crack. "What will you do with Simon when you go back to work?"

Olivia came to stand beside the rocking chair, looking over his shoulder at her son. She smelled like baby powder, a fragrance that should be anything but arousing. Unfortunately, Daniel couldn't quite convince his libido of that.

"Well," she said, oblivious to his discomfort, "that's one good thing about Seton General. They have a wonderful day-care facility on the premises. It's something the employees demanded for a long time and finally got last year. So I'll get to see Simon pretty frequently during the day. Sylvie's also insisting that she wants to sit with him two days a week, and since she works nights, that shouldn't put a hardship on her. If she still wants to do it when it's time for me to go back to work, I'm perfectly willing to let Simon spend a couple days a week with his auntie."

The baby in Daniel's arms responded to the sound of his mother's voice, squirming and jerking his legs and arms about fitfully. Realizing Simon needed something he couldn't provide—namely breakfast—Daniel rose from the chair and carefully handed the infant to Olivia, who took the seat he vacated and promptly began to unbutton her nightgown.

"Well, if you ever need me to watch him," Daniel said as he turned away, "I'll be happy to."

He was already out the door when Olivia said thanks. Mumbling a quick "Don't mention it," he headed downstairs to see what he had on hand for a more adult breakfast. After feeding himself and Olivia, he'd run next door to see just how extensive the damage was to her house. Because the sooner he could get her and her son moved back there, he decided, the sooner he'd be able to regain whatever shaky peace of mind he'd had before. Before he'd seen her looking beautiful and rumpled sleeping in his bed. Before he'd held her son and wondered what it would be like to have a child of his own someday. Before he'd realized how perfect it felt for the three of them to be together on a sunny Saturday morning.

Olivia watched him leave with something akin to relief and wondered at her reaction. She had never before found Daniel's presence to be anything other than comfortable. Since he had moved in next door two years ago, what had begun as idle chatting over the fence had gradually built into a fairly close friendship. They often acted as each other's rescuers, whether the threat in question was a stalled car, a flooded basement or a missing book. She confided in him when bits of her life seemed to be straying from plan, and even if he had no sound advice to offer her, he commiserated with her over lunch. Somehow he always seemed to make her feel better about things.

Daniel was her friend. He was her confidant. Her pal. So why all of a sudden did his mere presence in the same room make her feel uncomfortable? Why was he looking at her as if she were something worth looking at? Why had she had such erotic dreams last night, the focus of which had been none other than her next-door neighbor?

She looked down at the baby who was still feeding hungrily and smiled. "I hate to tell you this, kiddo, but your mommy's a crazy lady," she said softly.

Simon made a contented sound as he flexed his fingers and toes.

She placed a brief kiss on his downy head before continuing. "Mommy doesn't seem to know up from down lately. She's beginning to think her buddy Daniel is something he's not. She's beginning to think he's yummy. And she knows better than that, Simon. She certainly knows better than that."

Olivia had never had a relationship with a man that hadn't left her hurting in some way. Never. Not until Daniel McGuane. He was the first man who had never made her feel like less of a person, the first man who had left her consistently feeling good. And the only reason she could think of to explain that phenomenon was the fact that Daniel was her friend and not her lover. Becoming sexually involved with someone always seemed to mess things up, she reflected. And what she shared with Daniel was too nice to mess with. So she was just going to have to get her erotic dreams about him under control.

"Too much hormonal activity," she told Simon as she switched him from one breast to the other. "That's Mommy's problem right now. Before the end of the year, everything will be back to normal—you just wait and see. You'll be weaned, Mommy's hormones will be settled down, she'll have lost all this weight she picked up bringing you into the world and she'll go back to seeing Daniel as just her friend."

Olivia sighed as she concluded her reassurance. Deep down, she knew that with Simon's arrival, *normal* would take on an entirely new meaning. Still, there was no reason her relationship with Daniel had to change, was there? What she had with him was fine exactly the way it was. She wasn't about to blow a perfectly good friendship by allowing her completely unfounded—and no doubt completely temporary—sexual interest in him to get out of control.

And that should be easy enough to accomplish, she decided quickly, seeing as how Daniel McGuane had nothing in common with the men she normally dated. He was too quiet, too calm, too settled, too nice. There was no element of danger about him, no risk factor involved. Where was the challenge of going after a guy like him? Where was the fun?

"Daniel is Mommy's friend," Olivia reiterated resolutely to her son. "And friends are too important to lose. So

let's both do our best to maintain the status quo, okay, Simon?''

Simon pushed himself away from her breast with a yawn
and moved his head slowly from side to side. If she hadn't
known better, she would have sworn her son was refusing to
go along with her plan. Of course, she knew that was ridiculous. He couldn't even hold his head up, let alone shake it
in disagreement. Still, he seemed to have a funny little gleam
in his eyes....

"Oh, don't be silly," Olivia instructed herself out loud.
She settled the baby against her shoulder and rubbed his
back, telling herself she must be out of her mind. Things
would go back to normal, she assured herself again. Unfortunately, she had no idea what normal was going to wind up
being.

Actually, the damage to Olivia's house wasn't nearly as
bad as Daniel had first surmised. The whole back porch
would have to be rebuilt, naturally, but the foundation itself was still perfectly stable so that it would only be a matter of erecting new walls and a roof. All of her plants were
goners, though, he thought with a sad shake of his head as
he looked down at the limp greenery scattered everywhere.
Even Olivia, with her green thumb, could do nothing about
those.

He couldn't prevent the shudder that wound through him
at the knowledge of what else might have been lost. But
Olivia and the baby were fine, he reminded himself, safely
ensconced within the walls of his home, right where they—

He stopped the thought before it could be concluded. No,
the two of them did not *belong* in his home, he told himself. Hell, his home was barely fit for his own habitation, let
alone equipped for the needs of a newborn. Olivia's house
provided a far better environment for raising a child. There
was comfort here. Love. Two things patently missing from
his own house. And after seeing the change that had come
over the place this morning by the simple addition of mother

and child, he knew he was kidding himself if he thought any amount of home improvement he could physically create would manifest itself in the kind of atmosphere he had witnessed a short time ago.

He'd been kidding himself about a lot of things, he supposed.

"How does it look?"

He turned to find a barefoot Olivia crossing the yard between their houses. He was thankful to see that she now wore shapeless sweatpants and an oversize T-shirt sporting the logo of a popular Wildwood bar. As usual, she cradled Simon in her arms, and the baby squinted his eyes against the glare of a sun that had by now risen well into the sky.

"You're going to have to get him a little pair of baby sunglasses," Daniel remarked with a chuckle when he saw the infant's reaction.

Olivia laughed, too. "They actually make them, you know. They're about this big." She held up her free hand, drawing her index finger as far from her thumb as it would go, then tucked it under Simon again. "You'd be amazed at the things they make for babies. All in very tiny sizes."

"Well, at least you won't have to worry about buying the little nipper a new house," he told her. "You're going to need a new back porch, of course, but there's no danger to the rest of the structure. Your insurance will cover the cost of the repairs."

Olivia breathed a sigh of relief. She wasn't sure how she could have managed if the tree limb had done serious damage. Not the expense, seeing as how her insurance would cover it, but where would she stay while the work was going on? Daniel's? Not bloody likely. Not with her hormones betraying her every step of the way.

"You're certain my insurance will pay for it?" she asked.

He nodded. "No problem. I can give you a good reference for a guy who'll be able to do the reconstruction for you. He works cheap for friends and friends of friends."

She smiled. "Sounds like my kind of guy."

Daniel smiled back. "Great. I can start Monday."

Olivia's smile fell. "You?"

"Well, this is kind of what I do for a living, you know."

"I know, but... But will you have time? I mean, aren't you in the middle of a project for someone else right now?"

He shook his head, his sandy hair falling over his forehead with the gesture. When he swept it back, his eyes held a suspicious look. "As a matter of fact, I'm currently between jobs, and this one won't take that long. I can have your porch back up and good as new in a few weeks. What's the matter, Livy? Don't you have faith in my work? I can give you plenty of references—"

"No, that's not it at all," she assured him. "It's just—"

"What?"

What indeed? Olivia asked herself. She knew Daniel was good at what he did. His carpentry skills were in great demand, and he was never out of work unless he wanted to be. He'd be especially careful in rebuilding her porch because he cared about her and Simon. He was going to charge her a competitive rate for which her insurance company would pay. So what was the problem?

"Okay," she finally agreed, uncertain why she should feel so reluctant to do so.

"Is it all right if I get an early start on Monday morning?" he asked. "Say around seven?"

She nodded, still uncomfortable with the arrangement, but not sure why. "I'm always up before then with Simon."

Daniel glanced over his shoulder at the huge limb still sprawled across the remnants of her porch. "Got a chain saw?" he asked.

Olivia shook her head.

"That's okay. I have one. Might as well go to work on the limb this afternoon, if it's okay with you. I've got nothing better to do. I'll stack the logs by your garage. They'll come in handy this winter."

And with that, Daniel spun on his heel and headed for his own house. When he returned he was carrying a chain saw in one hand and a galvanized trash can in the other, a pair of safety goggles dangling over one wrist. He placed his heavier burdens near the crushed back porch, then reached behind himself to bunch his T-shirt in one hand. Olivia watched in fascination as he pulled it over his head and tossed it to the ground, then tied a tightly wound red bandanna around his forehead. When he stood before her in nothing but his work boots and jeans, she remembered suddenly why this arrangement wasn't going to work.

Daniel McGuane, she decided then, was just too yummy for words.

Three

———

Olivia awoke early Monday morning not to the raucous howl of a chain saw, but to a steady, muted *thump* ... *thump* ... *thump* that penetrated her weary brain a little bit at a time. She rolled to her side and squinted at the digital clock on her nightstand to find that it was nearly seven-thirty, then bolted up out of bed and across the hall to the nursery to check on Simon, alarmed that the baby hadn't awakened her sooner. She had last fed him shortly after 3:00 a.m., and he'd never gone this long without eating. Yet she found him sleeping peacefully in his crib, looking unbelievably small on the minuscule mattress, surrounded by toys almost as big as himself. He lay on his stomach, his fingers curled into two tiny fists on each side of his head, oblivious to the turmoil that rolled around inside her.

Olivia sighed her relief and smiled. This motherhood business was unlike anything she'd ever experienced, and she wasn't sure she was ever going to get used to it. She'd never had to worry about another human being before. Heavens, she'd scarcely ever bothered to worry about herself. Now Simon—a tiny baby who would be in no way capable of looking after himself for years—seemed to be at the forefront of every thought she had, and was indeed the focus of her entire day. Without even thinking about the gesture, she reached down and stroked her finger gently over his cheek, smiling again when he yawned and nodded his head toward her hand in his sleep.

Outside the nursery, the steady thumping that had awakened her continued—more loudly than it had been in her own room—and Olivia moved to the window that looked out over the backyard. The back porch still lay in a pile of broken wood below her to her right, though she and Daniel had cleaned up much of the mess during the two days that had passed since the storm. Beyond the remnants of her porch, alongside her garage, an impressive store of firewood had begun to collect. The huge branch that had fallen three nights before was gradually dwindling to a pile of logs and kindling thanks to Daniel McGuane, who, she noted, was pretty close to disposing of it entirely.

He stood in the center of her backyard, stripped to the waist as he had been Saturday morning. Wound around his head was a blue bandanna nearly as faded as his scruffy jeans. He was swinging an ax in a rhythmic motion, slowly lifting it in a high arc above his head before bringing it crashing back down to splinter a log in two. Although he stood in the shade of a towering sugar maple, the sunlight fell upon him in dappled bits of light, glinting off a thin sheen of perspiration that glistened on his muscular torso. Olivia wondered how long he'd been out there working this morning without her knowing.

When she lifted a hand unconsciously to her throat, she felt the pulse of her blood running rampant through her veins. Although the morning breeze sifting through the open window was cool, she suddenly felt very warm. She wasn't sure just how long she stood there enjoying the sight of

Daniel so concentrated on his work, but when Simon finally stirred, she found it difficult to pull her attention away. Finally, when the baby let out a howl to communicate more adamantly that his needs were being neglected, Olivia turned away from the window.

But not before Daniel looked up to discover that she was watching him.

Quickly, awkwardly, she lifted a hand in greeting, fighting back the blush she felt heating her chest and face. She hastened away from the window, wondering what madness had come over her to become so thoroughly enthralled with the simple sight of a man performing physical labor. It wasn't like she'd never seen a man's chest before, she reminded herself as she lifted the baby from his crib, took her seat in the rocking chair and pushed aside her gown so that he could feed. She was a mother, after all, and therefore obviously sexually experienced. Steve had been a very attractive man physically, she recalled. But she couldn't remember once sitting and staring at him the way she had just shamelessly inventoried Daniel McGuane.

"Hormones," she said to her son as he suckled hungrily, his eyes never leaving hers. The word seemed to have become a litany over the past few days. "It's just Mommy's overactive hormones. It's all your fault, you know," she told the baby with an affectionate smile, touching her finger lightly to his nose. "My body's completely out of shape because of you."

Glancing down at her ample waist and down farther at the thighs peeking out from the hem of her nightie—thighs she scarcely recognized as her own—Olivia sighed more deeply. If she ever hoped to wear anything in her closet again, she was going to have to lose some weight.

"That's my big boy," she said quietly when Simon finished with his breakfast, pushing his face away from her breast. She lifted him to her shoulder and rubbed a hand softly over his back, waiting patiently while he took his time to burp. When he did, she chuckled, once again marveling at the life she had created, the life for which she alone would be responsible. When she cradled him in her arms again, she gazed down at him, and Simon stared intently back, as if he found her the most fascinating thing on earth to study.

"I don't know about this, kiddo," she said, curling his four fingers and thumb over her single index finger. "You're looking at me like you think I know what to do next, and frankly, Simon, nothing could be farther from the truth. I'm no more certain of the steps we're supposed to follow than you are. So you're going to have to help me out here. Give me a sign or something. It's a good thing there's two of us to figure this stuff out, because two is none too many."

He seemed to have complete faith in her, she thought as he continued to watch her, tightening his fingers lightly around hers. Boy, did she have him snowed. Of course, he was only a little baby right now and didn't know any better, she told herself. What was she going to do as he aged and began to figure things out? Eventually he was bound to re-alize that there was something missing from his life—namely, a father. What was she going to do when he did? How was she going to explain things to him then? How was she going to make up for such a significant missing piece?

"Olivia? It's Daniel. Are you up?"

The voice came from downstairs, and Simon turned his face toward it even before she did. She eyed the baby sus-piciously. She could have sworn her new mother books had said that three weeks old was too early for a baby to smile in response to something, but she'd be darned if this wasn't the second time her son had done just that at the mention of Daniel McGuane's name.

"I'm in the nursery," she called out as she readjusted her gown to cover herself. "Come on up."

She stood and shifted Simon to her shoulder again, turn-ing toward the sound of footsteps on the aged, creaky stairs. After a moment, Daniel poked his head around the nursery door, his face a silent question mark, as if he felt he were

intruding. When Olivia smiled a welcome and turned so that
the baby could see him, too, he came into the room.

His bandanna was gone, and his sweat-soaked hair hung
in damp spikes over his forehead. He had shrugged into a
chambray shirt dotted with a few small rips and streaks of
what looked to be grease, its faded blue nearly identical to
the color of his eyes. But he'd left the shirt unbuttoned, and
she still had a very clear, very nice, view of the naked flesh
beneath. His chest was smooth, tanned and completely de-
void of hair, something she found surprising. And surpris-
ingly erotic, she thought further, recalling that all of the men
she'd ever dated had been dark and very, well...hairy.

"Hi, little guy," he said to the baby as he entered the
nursery, bending to bring his eyes level with Simon's when
he stopped behind the two of them.

She felt the baby squirm happily in her arms and smiled.
"He likes you," she said.

When Daniel's eyes met hers, she could see that he was
surprised and delighted by her statement. "Really? How can
you tell?"

"He always wiggles like this when he sees you or hears
your voice. And he always seems to smile whenever I say
your name in front of him."

Daniel looked back at the baby, but he was still clearly
speaking to Olivia when he said, "So, you two have been
talking about me, eh? I can only wonder what you've been
saying."

She could have kicked herself for what she'd just revealed, and she tried to recover for her gaff by remarking,
"Oh, this and that. I had to explain what that strange noise
was outside, didn't I? And who that man was in the bedroom the other morning, right?"

Simon wiggled again, stretching an arm over her shoulder as if reaching toward Daniel. With a quiet laugh, Daniel touched his finger to the baby's. "I see. Well, little guy,
get used to me. Because I'm going to be around a lot for a
while."

She knew he'd only said it in terms of fixing her back porch, but his reassurance to her son that he would be present in her home for some time to come was comforting to Olivia, too. When he straightened up, she felt oddly cheated by his withdrawal, but his smile—a smile that was clearly meant for her alone—made her feel a little better.

"And hi to you, too," he said softly. She got the impression he would always speak softly in the presence of the baby, whether Simon was sleeping or not.

"Good morning," she told him. "Simon has just finished his breakfast, so he's a fat, happy baby. How about you? Have you eaten?"

Daniel nodded. "I've been up since six, and since I'm going to be putting in a full day, I had a big breakfast. Oatmeal, half a cantaloupe, a couple of corn muffins, a big glass of OJ..."

Olivia wrinkled her nose. "Healthy stuff," she said.

He nodded again.

"I was going to offer you a bowl of Cocoa Puffs, but since you've already eaten..."

He chuckled. "Thanks anyway."

"Would you mind keeping an eye on Simon for me while I go get dressed?"

Daniel was helpless not to notice the length of bare leg that extended for what seemed like miles from the hem of her gown to the floor. He sighed inwardly. Did she have to get dressed? he wondered. Couldn't she just wear that for the rest of the day? The rest of her life? She was probably going to go brush her hair, too, he thought morosely, and tame down that wonderful, sleep-rumpled riot of curls.

As if she could detect his thoughts, she ran her hand restlessly through her hair, bunching it in a fist at her nape before releasing it. All he could do was wish it was his own hand performing the gesture instead, and almost instinctively his fingers curled into fists at his side.

"Sure," he said, forming the reply reluctantly. "I'd love to keep an eye on Simon while you get dressed."

She handed him the infant with a grateful smile, then brushed past as if she were completely oblivious to the sexual heat burning up the air between them. Which of course, he realized, she was. Olivia Venner was no more aware of the anxious need winding through his body than she was of the earth's rotation. And like the earth's rotation, his desire for her was something that would always be there, a fact of life that would never change. It just wasn't something she ever gave a thought to.

The baby in his arms cooed and squirmed, and Daniel's attention wandered from Simon's mother to Simon. He still couldn't get over how small the little guy was, couldn't believe anything so tiny would someday grow into a man. He still marveled at the fact that Olivia had created and nurtured this human being inside of her for months. He admired her for the task she had taken on in raising a child alone. He wished there were some way—

No, he didn't, he assured himself quickly, looking away from Simon's intent scrutiny. He did *not* wish there was some way he could help her out. Olivia Venner's family life was none of his business, something she had made clear since the beginning of their friendship. Not that she had ever been mean or nasty to him—there was just something in her demeanor that let others know she was more than capable of taking care of things herself. At least, he amended, *she* was convinced she could take care of things herself.

He only wondered if that certainty in her extended to little Simon, as well. Since she'd come home from the hospital with the baby, there had been times, brief moments, when she didn't seem to be quite as confident with her son as she normally was with herself. Sometimes, when Daniel snuck peeks at her he didn't think she noticed, she looked almost...lost. And at times like those, he couldn't help but wonder and wish—

Don't do it, he cautioned himself. Don't start getting soft, fuzzy thoughts about Olivia or her baby. She was an independent woman who had been taking care of herself for years, and who would continue on quite capably without him or anyone else interfering.

Still, he couldn't help but wonder...

"Daniel?"

He turned abruptly at the sound of her voice coming from the opposite side of the hall. "Yes?"

"Could you hang around inside with the baby for a little while longer? I'd love to take a shower."

He squeezed his eyes shut at the image her words evoked in his already muddled brain. She'd had to say it. She'd had to say something like that, something totally innocuous to her way of thinking, but something that set him on his ear with the image of her naked and warm and wet.

When he didn't reply right away, she appeared at the nursery door wearing a short robe. Instinctively, he knew she was completely naked beneath it, knew that all he'd have to do was unhitch the loose knot at her waist and pull her forward to bury his head between her breasts. She'd be warm and fragrant, her skin satiny smooth, and she'd taste like a rich, ripe—

"Daniel?" she said again, her expression puzzled, no doubt as a result of his lack of communication.

"Hmm?" The quick murmur was all he was able to manage.

"Would it be too inconvenient to watch Simon for a few more minutes? I'll hurry."

"Sure," he told her, his voice sounding strained and strangled, even to his own ears. He cleared his throat and strove for steadiness as he garbled out further, "No problem. And don't rush. I don't mind taking a break for a little while. I'm at a good stopping place anyway."

She smiled, and something hot and heavy settled over his heart, sinking down into his gut like a blacksmith's anvil.

"You're sweet," she said as she vanished again. But her voice lingered after her disappearance. "Thanks. I owe you big for all these favors, Daniel. Whatever I can do to make it up to you, just name it."

He opened his mouth to name something she would most certainly consider inappropriate, and quickly snapped it shut again. There was a child present, after all, he reminded himself as he glanced down at the baby in his arms again. And children were just so damned impressionable.

When Olivia came downstairs a half hour later, freshly showered and dressed in yet another pair of sweatpants and yet another oversize T-shirt, she headed immediately to the kitchen to appease her rumbling stomach. Daniel probably thought she'd been joking about those Cocoa Puffs earlier, she reflected as she pulled a box of the cereal from a cabinet and dumped a generous portion of it into a bowl. She splashed on some milk and lifted an overflowing spoonful to her mouth. It was amazing what a sweet tooth she'd developed while she was expecting. Not that she'd ever shunned sweets before, but something about being pregnant had just made sweets seem so...so...so terribly necessary.

She looked out the kitchen window into the backyard as she shoveled another spoonful of cereal into her mouth, then paused in midcrunch when she saw Daniel and Simon outside. The larger of the two males was seated in a lounge chair holding the smaller in his lap, and he was talking to the infant as if conversing with a three-week-old was something he did every morning. She smiled. She'd love to know what Daniel was saying, would love to know how Simon was responding. Hurriedly, she finished up her breakfast, rinsed the dishes and settled them in the dishwasher, then headed out the back door.

She tried to be as quiet as possible as she snuck up on the pair, straining to hear what they were talking about. Unfortunately, Daniel must have sensed her arrival, because he turned abruptly when she was still a good ten feet away from him, smiled guiltily and flushed with panic.

"Uh, I was just telling Simon about the cardinal family you have nesting in your crepe myrtle," he said. "The little guy's been on the edge of his seat listening to me. I think he's going to be an ornithologist when he grows up."

Olivia grinned. "Already filling him in on the birds and the bees, huh? Boy, you guys really do start early."

Daniel blushed more furiously, and her smile broadened. She didn't think she'd ever seen a man blush before, and she found the reaction oddly appealing.

"No, of course not," he said. "He's way too young to hear about...about...you know...about stuff like *that.*"

She drew nearer, watching the baby on his lap as Simon's gaze fixed intently on Daniel. "I'm not so sure," she said, her voice touched with melancholy. "They say you should explain all that to your kids as soon as they're old enough to even vaguely understand. It's kind of sad, really, how much you have to tell children as soon as they're old enough to understand. Seems like they should stay innocent forever."

"The world's a different place than it was when you and I were kids," Daniel told her.

She curled Simon's fingers over her own, a gesture he could see gave her some small amount of comfort. "I know. And in a lot of ways, it's a better place. But...I just...I don't know." When her eyes met his, they were filled with something he could only liken to anxiety. "I just worry about him, you know?"

Daniel nodded. "That's understandable, Livy. And perfectly natural."

She warmed at the sound of her nickname on his lips again. Her gaze shifted to Simon's hand on her own; then she looked up to meet Daniel's gaze more fully. "I worry most about him not having a father around."

Daniel felt his heart rate quicken at the way she was looking at him. He told himself he was only imagining things, assured himself there was nothing in Olivia's statement that involved him in any way. Nevertheless, she had a funny look in her eye.

"It doesn't seem fair to him," she continued without waiting for him to reply. "I know that's old-fashioned, and I know plenty of perfectly normal, healthy children are raised by their mothers alone, but it doesn't seem right somehow. A child should have two parents. Period. Two people who can turn to each other in a time of need, who can present a united front or a variety of points of view. A little boy especially needs a man he can look up to, a man to emulate, a man who—"

She stopped abruptly and looked away, and he knew at once that she had revealed more about her fears than she had intended.

"I'm sorry," she said quickly, still not looking at him. She chuckled nervously. "I don't know what's making me so philosophical and socially aware this morning. Guess I stayed in the shower too long. My brain must be water-logged."

"Or maybe you're just learning what it is to be a mother," Daniel told her.

She did look at him then, smiling gratefully that he didn't think her a complete idiot for rambling on the way she had. She nodded briefly, and reached for Simon, no longer able to tolerate not having him close. The baby studied her for a moment, then his eyelids began to descend over his eyes. As hard as he fought to maintain consciousness, it was only a moment before he fell asleep.

When Olivia looked up at Daniel again, it was to find him watching not the baby, as she had been, but her. Closely, speculatively. With a quickly muttered excuse, she hurried back to the house to put Simon down for a nap.

As she stood over his crib watching him sleep, she heard the sound of Daniel's ax splitting more logs outside, and she gripped the rails of the crib to keep herself from moving to the nursery window to watch him. Every instinct inside her commanded that she go outside to him. She could tell him she just wanted to help out, just wanted to offer her services and do whatever she could to make his task move along more quickly.

It made sense, she thought. The sooner she could get Daniel out of her yard and out of her house, the sooner she could rid herself of this ridiculous attraction that had come up out of nowhere and made no sense at all. Then she could go back to seeing him the way she always had—as her neighbor, her buddy, her friend.

But as she moved toward the window and looked down into the backyard to watch him work, a coil of heat began to wind tighter and tighter somewhere low in her midsection. All Olivia could do was sit and wait, and wonder when it was all going to come undone.

Four

"**Y**ou realize, of course, Livy, that you're living out every woman's fantasy here."

Olivia turned away from the cup of tea she was brewing at the kitchen counter and eyed her little sister, Sylvie, skeptically. "Oh, sure. I'm a single mother who's temporarily without income, whose bank account is dwindling quickly and whose future is wide open and impossible to make plans for. I worry constantly not only about myself, but about a child I'm completely responsible for and still getting used to—that's every woman's fantasy all right."

Sylvie sat on the opposite side of the room at the table and ignored her sister's outburst, instead hovering over her infant nephew as he lay in his busy bouncer that now replaced the lazy Susan at the table's center. She shook a soft rattle over Simon's head, laughing at his expression as he tried awkwardly to reach for it and missed by a mile. "I guess motor skills are mastered a lot later than five weeks," she said.

"Evidently," Olivia agreed as she moved to join her sister at the table. "Although he's doing better all the time. At least he's not crossing his eyes as much as he used to. He hardly looks anything like Buddy Hackett anymore."

"Still no hair, though," Sylvie said, stroking her palm carefully over the nearly nonexistent fuzz that covered Simon's head. "Then again, that's not such a bad thing, either. Some of your sexiest leading men are bald. Yul Brynner, Telly Savalas, that guy who plays Captain Picard on 'Star Trek.' Not to mention Mr. Clean, of course."

Olivia paused as she pulled the tea bag from her cup and squeezed out the excess with her fingers. She placed the limp bag on her saucer and reached for the sugar bowl. "You think Mr. Clean is sexy?"

"Oh, absolutely," Sylvie said enthusiastically. "Those big muscles and that tight, white T-shirt. And who do you think made this earrings-for-men trend so fashionable?"

Olivia nodded as she pondered that, then recalled how her sister had started this conversation. "So what's this fantasy I'm living that you were going on about?"

Sylvie gestured over her shoulder toward the back door. "That unbelievably scrumptious, nearly naked man who's been hanging around your place for the last two weeks, that's what."

Olivia glanced quickly toward the back door, then threw her sister a censorious glare. "Will you keep your voice down?" she whispered. "He might hear you."

Sylvie shrugged, clearly unconcerned. "Hey, *I* don't care if Daniel McGuane knows I think he's sexy as all get-out. *You're* the one who has a problem acknowledging your feelings."

"I do *not* have a problem acknowledging my feelings," Olivia assured her. "And my feelings where Daniel is concerned happen to be very mild. He's a nice guy. Period. And in no way, shape or form my type."

Her sister uttered a rude sound of disbelief. "Oh, please, Livy. I saw the way you looked at him a little while ago when he came in for a drink of water. Have you been lusting after him this way ever since he started working for you?''

"You're imagining things, as usual, little sister. I have not been lusting after Daniel McGuane. Ever. He's not..."

"Yeah, yeah, I know. Not your type." She sighed wistfully. "Jeez, but how can you stand it having him here every single day, looking like... like..." She lifted a hand to her forehead as if warding off a fever. "Like *that*. I mean, how do keep yourself from jumping his bones the second he comes through the door?"

Olivia's stomach knotted at the image her sister's words evoked. Not a day had gone by in the past two weeks when she hadn't involuntarily experienced thoughts exactly like what Sylvie was suggesting. Having Daniel McGuane in her home was a lot different from having him safely ensconced next door where she could say hello to him in passing and then put him out of her mind.

Every weekday morning for the past two weeks, he had arrived at her back door, greeted her with that maddeningly sexy smile, stripped off half of his clothes to reveal an unbelievably well-toned body and gone to work. What sane woman wouldn't be driven mad by such behavior? And the weekends, when he hadn't even been around, had been far worse, because she spent her Saturdays and Sundays wondering what he was doing, and with whom he was doing it, and impatiently waiting for Monday morning to roll around so that she could see him again.

"See?" Sylvie taunted. "You're blushing. I knew you had the hots for Daniel."

"Shh!" Olivia hissed. "I am not blushing. It's the heat from the stove and the tea. And I do not have the hots for Daniel," she added adamantly. "Quit trying to create a situation you know will never happen."

But instead of quieting, Sylvie changed her expression to one of utterly mischievous evil and shouted toward the back door, "Oh, Daniel! Could you come inside for a minute?"

Olivia narrowed her eyes at Sylvie, rising from her seat with every intention of strangling her little sister, hoping she could still manage that threatening tone of voice that had once scared the bejeebers out of her. "Sylvie, what do you think you're doing? I swear if you keep this up, I'll—"

"Yes?"

Daniel's voice preceded him by only a second, and Olivia dropped limply back down into her seat at the sight of him. He paused at the back door without entering, his damp chest and jeans covered by bits of sawdust and plaster. Perspiration streamed down his cheeks and chest, and for some strange reason, all Olivia could think about was how he would taste at that very moment. Hastily she tamped down the errant thought and went back to studiously preparing her cup of tea, shoveling a huge spoonful of sugar into the cup. Suddenly, however, something hot to drink was the last thing she wanted or needed.

"Sorry," Daniel went on when he noted her reaction. "I know I'm a mess."

When he swiped halfheartedly at the white powder that dotted his pectoral muscles, Olivia hoped no one besides herself heard the strangled little sound she couldn't control at witnessing the gesture. Unable to look away, she scooped up another spoonful of sugar and spent an inordinate amount of time stirring it into her tea.

"I'll try not to track all this into the house," he added as his hand swept lower.

Olivia stirred her tea more furiously, sloshing a good bit over the side of the rim without noticing.

"No problem," Sylvie told him with a.devilish smile when she noted her sister's reaction.

"What was it you needed?" Daniel asked.

Sylvie's smile broadened. "You know, all of a sudden, I can't for the life of me remember. Isn't that the silliest thing? I must be getting senile in my old age."

Olivia made a face at her. "Gee, Sylvie, last time I checked, most people didn't consider twenty-nine to be the age at which the onset of mental deterioration begins."

"Speak for yourself," Sylvie said. "You're almost thirty-three. What do you know? Your brain is probably Swiss cheese by now."

Olivia turned to Daniel and shook her head. "Kids."

He smiled. "I'm thirty-four," he told Sylvie. "So what does that make me?"

Olivia could see her sister biting her lip in an effort to keep herself from uttering a reply that would probably be indecent and would undoubtedly be embarrassing. Instead, Sylvie only said, "Um, mostly that makes you, uh, too old for me."

"I see," Daniel replied with a grin. "Well, when your decrepit brain remembers what it was you wanted, just give this old geezer a yell, okay?"

Olivia watched her sister inspect Daniel's backside as he turned and left, and she shook her head hopelessly. "Too old for you?" she asked. "Now what makes me think that was a big, fat lie? And what was all that business about calling him inside, to begin with?"

Sylvie sighed again before turning her attention back to her sister. "I just wanted to see your reaction and prove a point, that's all," she said with a smile. "The point being that you can't be in the same room with Daniel McGuane without turning into a pool of warm baby oil." Before Olivia could contradict her, she added quickly, "And okay, maybe age has nothing to do with anything. The fact is, as much as that guy toasts my melbas, he really isn't my type at all."

Olivia decided it might be best to let the first part of Sylvie's statement go by without commenting and simply replied, "Oh? And just what type of man is your type?"

Sylvie arched her brows philosophically. "My type…my type is the invisible man. Frankly, I don't want one in my life in any way, shape or form. Men are pretty annoying creatures when you get right down to it."

"That doesn't keep you from going out with them by the legions," Olivia pointed out.

Sylvie shrugged. "Yeah, well, as annoying as they are, there are times when they can still be kind of amusing. In their own...childlike...kind of way."

"Mmm, hmm."

Sylvie glanced down at her watch and stood. "Oh, boy, I have to get out of here. I have some errands to run before I go to work tonight." She leaned over and kissed the crown of Simon's head. "Remember, I get to watch him on Mondays and Wednesdays after you go back to work, right?"

"Right."

"And if you ever need a baby-sitter for some other occasion, you know who to call."

Olivia took an idle sip of her tea and grimaced at how sweet it was. How had that happened? she wondered. She swallowed reluctantly before replying, "What other occasion would I possibly need a baby-sitter for? I don't have to go back to work for more than two months. Enjoy your freedom while you can, because I definitely intend to take advantage of you soon."

This time Sylvie wiggled her eyebrows suggestively. "Maybe it will be sooner than you think. You never know when some hunky guy will ask you out."

Olivia expelled a single, brief chuckle, but there wasn't an ounce of humor in the sound. She dropped her hands to her waist as she said, "No hunky guys are going to look twice if I don't drop some of this baby fat."

Sylvie rounded the table and bent to kiss her sister's cheek. "Oh, I don't know about that. I think you look pretty good with the extra weight. You always were too skinny. What were you before you got pregnant, about a size four?"

"A size two," Olivia replied wistfully.

Sylvie shook her head. "Two? Size two? Here's a news flash for you, Livy. No normal woman is a size two. The Stepford Wives *maybe* were a size two. That's a size that was only invented by misogynist fashion designers in the first place to make women feel guilty about not staying six-year-old girls forever. So what size are you now?"

"Eight," Olivia told her, wrinkling her nose in disgust.

Sylvie's chin dropped toward her chest. "*I'm* a size eight. That's *not* fat, you geek."

"But I'm smaller boned than you. I take after Mom. She was very petite."

Sylvie shook her head again. "You look terrific as a size eight. Nice and healthy for a change. Quit whining."

"You're out of your mind," Olivia told her. "I'm thirty pounds heavier now than I was going into this pregnancy thing."

Sylvie shrugged. "So why don't you ask Deltoid Dan out there if you can come over and borrow his weight-lifting equipment some time?" she asked. "Heck, he's so healthy, he could probably be your personal fitness trainer." She smiled lasciviously as she added, "If you asked him nicely."

Olivia frowned at her.

Sylvie threw up her hands in mock surrender. "Hey, Liv, I think you need him. And not just for the reasons *you* might think."

Olivia gave her sister a playful swat as she moved away. "Aren't you in a hurry to leave or something?"

"On my way out," Sylvie said as she exited with a wave.

Less than a moment after she disappeared through the door, Daniel showed up at it again. He wiped his hands on a dusty rag and stepped gingerly into the kitchen. His expression seemed a little worried as he asked Olivia, "Is everything okay? Sylvie said you needed me."

She nearly choked on the mouthful of tea she had just consumed, and slapped both hands over her lips to keep from spitting it out completely. When she was finally able to swallow, it was with some difficulty and followed by a fit of coughing. Immediately, Daniel was behind her, patting her back firmly as he pulled her hair away from her face.

Gradually, Olivia's sudden seizure subsided, and she was able to breathe easily—although somewhat feebly—once again. The cessation of her coughing, however, didn't lessen Daniel's attention. Even when she inhaled deeply and released the breath without difficulty, he continued to stroke her back and hold her hair in his hand. For a moment, she let him do it, allowed herself the simple self-indulgence of letting another human being come close.

He smelled good, she thought. Musky and redolent of the sunny afternoon. His hand was warm through the thin fabric of her T-shirt, the fingers tangling in her hair gentle and more than a little seductive. Seemingly of their own free will, her eyelids fluttered down over her eyes, and she began to lose herself in Daniel's touch.

But only until she realized how much she was enjoying herself. Then she snapped her eyes open again and leapt up from her chair, spinning around to face him and making every effort to tamp down the panic that threatened to grip her.

She paused when she surveyed Daniel, however. He sure had a funny expression on his face, she thought. His cheeks were flushed, and a corner of his mouth twitched once, ever so slightly. His eyes, normally the color of the clear sky outside, had darkened to the color of storm clouds, and he seemed suddenly angry about something.

"Thanks," she said, unable to think of anything else that might sufficiently defuse the situation. "I think I'm okay now."

He nodded, but his expression never altered.

"I don't know what came over me," she said, hoping her voice didn't sound as shaky as she felt. "I guess I just took too big a sip of my tea."

"Sylvie..." He stopped abruptly and cleared his throat before continuing. "Sylvie said you needed me," he repeated softly.

Olivia chuckled anxiously and tried to think fast. "I, um, yeah...I do. I, uh, I was wondering if you, ah, um...if you...if you wanted something to eat." Yeah, that's it, she thought. That sounded reasonable. "It's almost two o'clock, after all. Way past lunchtime. I was about to fix myself a sandwich. Would you like something?"

He looked at her for a moment before replying, and she suddenly wished she could tell what he was thinking. Then he lifted one shoulder in a half shrug, a motion she found fascinating because of the way it made the muscles in his upper torso dance. Heavens, it was suddenly getting warm in the kitchen, she thought. Had she forgotten to turn off the burner when she'd boiled the water for her tea?

"Sure," he said. "I am getting pretty hungry. A sandwich sounds good, if it's not too much trouble. Can I give you a hand?"

A hand? Olivia wondered vaguely as she stared at the ropes of sinew that wound down Daniel's upper arms. Yeah, a hand would be nice, for starters. She wouldn't mind if he gave her a few more pieces of his body, too, she thought further before she could prevent the idea from forming. Starting with his very intriguing—

"Olivia?" he asked when she showed no sign of replying to his question.

"Hmm?" she replied absently, still marveling at the craftsmanship that had gone into the creation of her next door neighbor.

"Can I give you a hand with lunch?" he repeated.

Eventually his question penetrated the feverish images burning into her brain, and she started visibly when she realized the direction her thoughts had taken.

"Oh," she said, feeling a little breathless for no reason she could name. Still, she admired herself for the quickness of her recovery when she continued, "Uh, yeah, okay. That would be nice."

"I'll just go outside and hose myself off first," he said, turning to leave.

Suddenly, Olivia didn't think she could tolerate it if Daniel was out of her sight for even a moment. "That's all right," she said, reaching her hand out to circle his wrist in an effort to keep him from leaving. He paused at her touch, turning to glance down at the delicate fingers wrapped around his lower arm. Slowly his gaze traveled from her hand up the length of her arm and shoulder, lingering at her throat, where she feared he could see the leap of her pulse as her blood hammered through her veins. Finally he focused on her face, but instead of meeting her eyes, he stared at her mouth, and instinctively, nervously, Olivia parted her lips.

His eyes met hers then, and she experienced the strangest feeling that something between the two of them changed at that very moment. She wasn't sure what or how or why, but *somehow*, suddenly, everything was different.

"You don't have to wash up outside," she said quietly, still not releasing his wrist. She could feel his pulse racing beneath her thumb and knew it only mimicked her own. "Just rinse off here at the sink. You're not that bad."

Not that bad. Daniel repeated the words in his head, over and over again until he managed to calm himself down. Regardless of the gentleness of Olivia's touch on his wrist, regardless of that lost, lonely look in her eyes and the wistful turn of her lips, regardless of what he thought she might be thinking right now, he had to remember that all in all, she would always think of him as *not that bad.* He was spinning dreams if he thought for a moment that her reluctance to have him go back outside was a result of anything other than her desire not to inconvenience him.

Nevertheless, he couldn't quite get over his reaction to Olivia's one, simple touch on his wrist. Her skin was warm and soft on his, seeming to melt into his flesh as if she were a part of him. She smelled like baby powder again, he noted as he inhaled on an unsteady breath, baby powder and something else that was still exclusively Olivia. Her hair hung in loose curls about her face, and all he wanted to do was bury his fingers in the unruly mass, then pull her face up to his and kiss her until the end of time.

Instead, he only nodded, mumbled his thanks and moved back toward the sink. While he washed up, he was conscious of the sounds of Olivia moving around behind him. While she paced back and forth between the refrigerator, counter and table, he sluiced the worst of the sawdust and plaster powder from himself, then dried off with a towel that appeared mysteriously beside him just as he was about to ask for one. When he finally turned around, he saw her on the opposite side of the table, slathering a generous portion of mayonnaise onto a slice of white bread. Involuntarily, he grimaced.

"You know, you really should avoid stuff like that," he said before he could stop himself.

She glanced up quickly, her expression almost panicked, as if she had forgotten he was there. "What stuff?" she asked.

"Mayonnaise, white bread. It's not good for you. And since you're still nursing Simon, you should try to stay as healthy as you can."

"Oh, no you don't," she said. "I was the model of nutrition while I was pregnant. I ate my five servings of fruits and vegetables every day, choked down my whole grains and my lean meats, and drank two—count 'em, *two*—big glasses of milk every day. And all in all, I'm still doing pretty well. But I've paid my dues. I deserve a reward every now and then." She pointed her knife at him menacingly. "If you think you're going to take my white bread away from me, mister, you've got another think coming."

He laughed, holding up his hands in surrender. "Okay, okay. Put down the knife. I'm sorry. Different strokes for different folks. I won't say another word about your eating habits."

"Thanks," she grumbled as she returned to her sandwich.

"Unless of course, you ask me about them."

She glanced up at him again, one eyebrow arched in silent question.

Daniel wasn't about to tell her he'd overheard her conversation with her sister earlier and her voiced concerns about her weight. He could only imagine what she'd say if she knew he'd been eavesdropping on the two of them. Actually, to be fair to himself, he hadn't been trying to eavesdrop. And they had to have known that he was working right outside the open back door, well within hearing range. How could he have missed what the two of them had been saying? As much as he wished he had. He hadn't needed to hear Olivia emphasize once again her unequivocal lack of interest in him. Although it was nice to know that Sylvie was in his corner. He needed all the help he could get.

"Is grape soda okay to drink?" Olivia asked him, and suddenly his thoughts were pulled back to the matter at hand. "Or I have some blue Kool-Aid I could mix up if you'd rather have that."

Daniel refrained from commenting and simply replied, "Ice water will be fine."

She nodded. "Would you rather have ham, meat loaf or turkey on your sandwich?"

"Turkey," he replied immediately. "With mustard, not mayo. And I don't guess you have any whole wheat bread, have you?"

Olivia wrinkled her nose in disgust. "I think there's still some in the freezer. I could toast it for you, I guess."

He smiled. "Thanks. I can do that when I get back. I'm going to go grab my shirt to put on."

He would have liked to think that the disappointed expression on her face was a result of her unwillingness to have him get dressed, but he was certain it was instead due to her distaste at his eating habits. Oh, well. He had a good reason for his life-style, and not even Olivia Venner could make him change his mind about that.

"I'll be right back," he said as he went to retrieve his chambray work shirt from the back porch.

"How's it coming out there?" she asked when he returned.

"Real well," he told her as he shrugged into the faded garment. He left it unbuttoned, however, since he'd be going back to work in a short time. "I'll be putting down the hardwood floor next week, and after a few more finishing touches, I should be about done. Start thinking about what color you want me to paint it."

"Wow, you work fast," she told him.

He shrugged. "Hey, it's my job."

And once it was over, he thought dismally, he'd be banished back to the sidelines of her life again. The realization bothered him a lot more than he'd thought it would. Hanging around with Olivia nearly every day for the past two weeks had been a joy. Seeing her come downstairs rumpled from sleep every morning, having her bring him a glass of juice or a cup of decaf had felt oddly right somehow.

He derived great pleasure in knowing that he was doing something for her, too, even if helping her out with the repairs to her home was something for which he was being paid. It *should* be him fixing her back porch, he thought, with or without remuneration. Because, dammit, as crazy as it sounded, he felt as if he belonged here with her.

Simon cooed when Daniel sat down near him, and he couldn't help but smile. The little guy had changed a lot since that first night Daniel had come barging into Olivia's house to make sure the two of them were okay with the storm raging outside. Daniel was amazed that a baby could change so quickly in such a short time. Simon was much bigger now, and he was beginning to resemble his mother quite a bit. When he smiled back at Daniel, Daniel laughed, chucking his finger under the baby's chin and receiving another smile in reward for the gesture.

"This is an awfully cute baby you've got here, Olivia," he said. He glanced up to find that she was watching him closely and had completely abandoned her preparation of lunch.

His comment seemed to snap her out of whatever reverie she'd been indulging in, however, because she shook her head once—quickly, as if to clear it—and went studiously back to work. "Uh, yeah," she said, her voice sounding a little rough. "Yeah, he is. He's a real sweetheart, too. He hardly ever cries, smiles a lot, loves to be held and he's unbelievably affectionate."

Daniel looked again at the baby in the bouncer, dropping his finger to the back of Simon's tiny hand, which wasn't much larger than the pad of Daniel's thumb. "You sound almost sad about that," he said.

She shrugged, but he could see that the gesture was anything but unconcerned. Her voice was quiet when she replied, "Maybe I am, a little."

"Why?"

She sighed deeply, hesitating a moment before she continued. "It's just...I don't know. Simon's so full of love, so responsive to me, I wonder sometimes if I'll be enough for him."

"Of course you'll be enough, Olivia. You're his mother."

"Even so, it seems unfair to try and raise him without a father. I don't care what anybody says—a little boy needs a man around to look up to. My father would have been a great role model if he were still alive, and my older brother, great guy that he is, only makes annual appearances in New Jersey, if that. I just can't help but feel that since Simon's not going to have a man around on a regular basis, he's going to be cheated out of so much."

"A lot of little boys grow up just fine with only their mothers," Daniel pointed out. He hoped he was able to keep the bitterness out of his voice when he added, "And having a man around the house is no guarantee that he's going to be a good role model or provide a good example of anything. There are plenty of fathers out there who never should have been allowed the privilege of the position. Some do more harm than good."

"I know," she agreed. But her mind seemed to be elsewhere, as if she were considering something other than the subject at hand. "It's just that there are specific 'Dad' jobs that I'm completely unprepared for."

"Like what?"

When she turned to look at him, she was smiling again, clearly remembering things now that made her happy. "Like... like packing the car for summer vacation. Dads always do that. My dad was the all-time champion of car packers. Taking the luggage for three kids and a wife who was in no way a light traveler, and getting everything in the trunk just so. He was an absolute engineer where packing a car was concerned." After a moment's thought, she added, "And jack-o'-lanterns."

Daniel narrowed his eyes in puzzlement at the quick change of subject. "Jack-o-'lanterns?"

She nodded. "Only dads seem to know how to properly eviscerate a pumpkin and turn it into a jack-o'-lantern at Halloween. My father was always the one to do that. I've never done it before. How am I supposed to teach Simon to do something like that?"

"You'll learn together," Daniel told her.

"I suppose.... But what about Christmas tree lights?"

"What about them?"

"Putting them on is a job for dads, too. So is making sure there are batteries in the spare flashlight, and... and taking the training wheels off bicycles, and explaining why the sky is blue and the grass is green. Who's going to do all those things for Simon? Who?"

Daniel reached across the table and covered her hand with his. "You will, Livy," he said simply. "And Simon will love you all the more because of it."

She sighed again, a desperate sound, and her eyes suddenly filled with tears. "You think so?" she asked softly.

He nodded. "Yeah, I do."

She turned her hand palm up and twined her fingers with his, a gesture she seemed to perform, he thought, as if she weren't even thinking about it. When her eyes met his again, they were a darker brown than he'd ever seen them, a result, he supposed, of the unshed tears.

"Daniel, I've been wondering if you could—"

She halted abruptly when she seemed to reconsider what she had been about to say, then pulled her hand out from beneath his. Hastily she swiped at her eyes, finished making his sandwich, then shoved the plate toward him without looking at him.

He waited to see if she would complete whatever question she had been about to ask, but it quickly became obvious she had no intention of doing that. So he waited patiently while she finished chewing the first bite of her own sandwich and then asked, "Could I what?"

"Never mind," she told him, still not looking at him. "It was a dumb idea. I couldn't impose on you like that."

"Like what?"

"Nothing," she said. "It's nothing. Forget I said anything."

"Olivia."

"What?"

"We've been friends for a long time now. You can ask me anything you want. Impose on me as much as you like. If it's too much of an imposition, I'll tell you so. Trust me."

Trust me. How many times had Olivia heard those words before, only to have them thrown right back in her face when she obliged? How many men had she trusted, only to be betrayed in the long run? Too many for her to count, she realized dismally. Too many for her to ever willingly trust one again. The funny thing was, though, she *did* trust Daniel. She always had. And somehow, she knew she always would. It was why she wanted to ask him the favor that had been bouncing around in her brain since Simon's birth.

"I was just thinking," she began again, surveying him nervously from beneath lowered lids.

"What?"

"If, someday, as Simon grows older . . ." she asked.

"Yes?"

"If he has some questions that I don't think I can answer, or if there's some kind of guy thing going on with him that I don't understand?"

"Mmm, hmm?"

"Would it be okay if...if I sent him over to talk to you?"

All the breath in Daniel's lungs left him in a whoosh. He couldn't have hidden his astonishment at her request if he had tried. All he could do was look first at Olivia, then at the tiny baby in the bouncer who stared back at him so curiously, then back at Olivia again. He didn't know what to say. What she was asking him to do was something he had never expected for a moment. She was entrusting him with her son. She was telling him she had enough regard for him to allow him some small measure of influence over her child. It both comforted and frightened him. And for the life of him, he didn't know what to say.

"Me?" he asked, the single-word reply all he was able to manage.

She nodded earnestly. "You're a good guy, Daniel. One of the few men I can think of who really seems to... to care about things. Does that make sense?"

"I guess so."

"If there were something Simon needed to know, something I couldn't help him out with, would you mind terribly if I told him to talk to you? I'll understand if you say no, of course. I guess it's a lot of responsibility, but I know he's going to look up to you. That's only natural. And with you being next door and all, I—"

"Yes," he said immediately. "It's okay."

She smiled, her relief evident. "Really? You don't mind?"

He shook his head, still a little dumfounded. "I don't mind. I'm flattered that you'd think enough of me to point Simon in my direction."

"Think enough of you?" she echoed his words. "Daniel, I... You can't even begin to imagine how much I think of you."

Her words mixed with the look in her eyes was all the encouragement he needed. Without thinking further, he rose from his seat and rounded the corner of the table, tugged Olivia up from her chair and pulled her into his arms.

Five

———

Daniel hesitated only a moment before kissing her, only long enough to let her stop him if she wanted to. But although her gaze locked earnestly with his and her lips parted ever so slightly, Olivia never uttered anything remotely resembling an objection. And when, instead of pushing him away, she wrapped her own arms around his waist, he bent to press his mouth against hers.

At first, he only brushed his lips lightly over hers, moving slowly to let them both get used to the sensation of being closer than they'd ever been before. But when that small gesture became intolerable, when it turned into a desperate need for more, he dragged her closer still, tangling his fingers in the hair at her nape as he bent her backward to plumb the depths of her mouth more fully.

Kissing Olivia was unlike anything Daniel could have ever imagined. He could feel the wild raging of her heart against his, was completely surrounded by the heat and fragrance of her. So charged did the air around them become, that he was certain he could actually feel their souls intermingling. As the fingers in her hair got lost in her softness, his other hand dipped lower, to the small of her back, urging her body closer to his.

At first, Olivia wasn't at all certain what had happened to her. She only knew that one moment she had been trying to tell Daniel what a good friend he was to her, and the next, she was caught up in some wild frenzy of wanting. He seemed to be everywhere—in front of her, beside her, behind her, inside her. Indeed, he seemed to be a part of her. She was on fire everywhere he touched her, from the crown of her head to the soft center of desire deep inside her. And however crazy she told herself what the two of them were doing was, she could no more stop herself from responding than she could stop the day from dawning.

The hand at her back traveled around to her front, dipping below the hem of her T-shirt to splay over the heated flesh of her torso beneath. She groaned at the exquisite sensations that shot through her, inflaming every cell in her body. Slowly Daniel's hand crept upward, hesitating at the lower swell of her breast. Without even realizing what she was doing, Olivia lifted her own hand to cover his, pushing his fingers up over the mound of her breast, gasping at the resulting fire that leapt up inside her and threatened to rage out of control.

At her insistence, he latched on to her more completely, skimming his fingertips over the soft cotton of her brassiere, raking his thumb over the rigid peak. He dropped his head to her throat, dotting the slender column with soft butterfly kisses that made her thoughts spin wildly around in her head. The hand at her nape fell to her derriere, pushing her toward the cradle of his thighs where she felt him ripening against her. Her eyelids fluttered shut at the erotic images that flickered to life in her fevered brain, and she cupped her own hand over him.

He growled from somewhere deep inside himself and nipped gently at the skin on her shoulder with his teeth before laving it over with his tongue. Olivia shivered at the primitive, almost bestial action, wondering faintly just how untamed and explosive a lover he would be if he completely lost control. Before she could ponder the idea further, he pushed at the neck of her T-shirt, trying to open it over her breast, tearing the fabric when it resisted. Then he was pushing her breast upward as his head descended, touching his tongue to the rise of pale flesh that curved above her brassiere.

"*Oh,*" she whispered as he caressed her. "Oh, Daniel."

In saying his name aloud, she was forced reluctantly to remember who he was, who she was, where they were and what they were doing. Immediately she sprang away from him, gripping the back of her chair to keep herself from crumbling into a quivering mass of nerves when her knees threatened to buckle beneath her. For long moments, she forgot to breathe; then she inhaled a deep, ragged gasp to jump-start her heart. Instinctively, she lifted her hand to her lips, but whether she was trying to dispel the feeling of his mouth against hers, or preserve the sensation forever, she wasn't sure. All she knew was that she had been kissing Daniel McGuane. Kissing him and more…and loving every minute of it. She couldn't understand her behavior.

"I'm sorry," she said quickly, quietly, her voice sounding shaky, even to her own ears. Though it wasn't clear, even to her, what she was sorry for.

For a moment, Daniel didn't reply, and she assumed it was because he was as astounded and confused as she was by what had just happened. She couldn't look at him, fearful that if she did, she would see a look of revulsion or worse on his face. All she could do was tug at her shirt to straighten it, stare down at the floor and wish he would say something. Finally he did.

"I'm not sorry," he told her. "Not for a minute."

She snapped her head up at that, even more confused than before. "But—"

He shook his head slowly, placing his finger gently against her mouth to halt the flow of words she felt erupting. "I'm not sorry," he said again. "Kissing you, holding you and more is something I've wanted to do for a long time. If you think I'm going to apologize for what just happened, you're out of your mind."

She covered his hand lightly with hers and removed his finger from over her lips. "Daniel," she began, "I...I don't know what to say. I'm not sure what just happened here. I...you...we..." She uttered an unsettling sound and tried again. "What...what happened?"

"I kissed you," he told her. "You kissed me back. And we both started to get a little crazy. That's what happened."

"But why?"

He smiled almost sadly. "Well, I'd like to think it was because of some mutual desire we have to get close to each other. Physically, mentally, spiritually, emotionally...in every way possible."

She shook her head. "But that's impossible. We're already close. Very close. We're close friends. But that's all we are."

"Yeah, well, maybe that's what we thought, but obviously we were mistaken about it."

She shook her head more fiercely. "No. I've never been more certain about my feelings where a man is concerned. You're a good friend, Daniel, and I don't want to mess that up." She lifted her hand to ward off the objection she could sense was coming. "And before you go into all that 'men-hate-it-when-women-say-let's-be-friends' business, let me point out that the two of us have been getting along just fine for two years with things between us at the friendly stage."

Speak for yourself, Daniel thought. He'd been a nervous wreck for the past two years, watching Olivia come and go from a distance, being a part of her life only on the fringe. Friends was the last thing he wanted to be with her. But he'd settled for that, because it was all she'd made available to him. And, hell, he'd been happy with it, too, up to a point. But now things were different between them.

Because now he'd held Olivia in his arms, had felt her respond to him in the most intimate way a woman could respond to a man. He'd had a small taste of what it would be like to make love to her. He also knew there was a lot more to her feelings for him than she was willing to admit. He knew he had a chance with her. A chance for something more than a good friendship. He'd be a fool if he let her retreat again after what they had just shared.

"Livy," he said, "you can't tell me that you didn't enjoy what just happened every bit as much as I did."

Her cheeks grew pink, her eyes darkened, and he knew she was about to tell him a whopper of a lie. "It was just..." she said. "You caught me off guard when you kissed me, that's all. And I just instinctively kissed you back. But there was nothing more to it than that."

"You're telling me you didn't feel anything out of the ordinary."

She flushed harder. "That's exactly what I'm telling you."

"What if I said I don't believe you?"

"Then I'd say you've got a monumental ego."

He smiled. "All right. We'll leave it at that. For now. But don't think this conversation is over. You and I still have plenty to talk about."

And with that, he took his plate and glass from the table and carried them out to the back porch, obviously intending to eat his lunch in solitude. Olivia was left alone with Simon, who stared at her intently as if demanding to know what she'd done to make Daniel McGuane go away. She opened her mouth to tell the baby it was none of his business, then closed it again with an anxious glance toward the back door. Taking her seat at the table again, she tore a hefty bite out of her sandwich and began to chew thoughtfully.

There was absolutely nothing more that she and Daniel needed to talk about, she assured herself. They had kissed. Big deal. Lots of good friends kissed now and then. Of course, she conceded, friendly-type kisses didn't usually result in some raging inferno of carnal desire, did they? Still, she hadn't been herself since Simon's birth. It had only been five weeks. No doubt that hormonal thing that had originally had her so concerned was still at play here. That's why she must have gotten so... heated up... by Daniel's embrace.

It had been a magnificent kiss, though, she thought further. Truly unlike anything she'd ever experienced before. Which just went to prove that what had happened was without question an aberration. Who ever got turned on like that when kissed by a friend? Nobody. Soon enough, her hormones would calm down, and everything would be back to normal.

As Olivia bit into her sandwich again, she told herself over and over that her life would settle down soon. She and Simon would fall into a routine, she would once again get involved in her work at the hospital and Daniel McGuane would go back to being her neighbor. But as easy as it was to comfort herself about the first two items in her reassurance, that last bit about Daniel simply wouldn't embed in her brain. Because she could still feel the soft brush of his lips against hers, could still taste the musky maleness of him on her tongue, could still smell the pungent aroma of fresh-cut wood that seemed to surround him, and she still grew warm at the memory of his soft touch on her breast.

And that, she decided, was probably going to make forgetting about this insignificant incident a little more difficult than she thought.

Olivia was still pondering the dilemma late that afternoon when Daniel found her in the laundry room catching up with a pile of Simon's washing.

"I'm at a good stopping place," he told her as he leaned laconically in the doorway.

She noted his leisurely posture from the corner of her eye and couldn't help but notice the way his open shirt displayed a number of his more prominent attributes. She decided immediately that it would probably be best if she didn't look up and get an eyeful of him head-on. "Fine," she said as she studiously continued to fold and refold Simon's little T-shirts and one-piece sleepers.

Daniel straightened, raising his arms above his head to lean against the doorjamb with more aplomb. She was certain he was intentionally trying to drive her mad by flexing a different series of muscles this time, and she hated herself for succumbing so completely to his ploy. Her heart seemed to simultaneously jump into her throat and plummet to her toes, and the air suddenly became far more oxygen-rich than it normally was. That was the only reason she could think of for why she would suddenly feel so woozy.

"So I thought I might knock off for the day," he added, "if it's all right with you. Unless you've got something else you want me to do for you."

"And what else could I possibly want you to do for me?" she asked, looking up to meet his gaze before she could stop herself.

Every drop of moisture evaporated from her mouth and throat when she saw him, and she knew she wouldn't be able to speak if she tried. The way he was standing in the doorway displayed every solid muscle in his torso and forearms with loving care, as if he were some prime piece of Greek-god sculpture. Dammit, why did he have to be so attractive? she wondered. And why hadn't she noticed it before so she could have prepared herself for this strange attraction a little better?

"Oh, I can think of one or two things," he said with a smile, never altering his pose.

She opened her mouth to deny that there was anything more she needed from him, then recalled that actually, there were one or two things she had considered earlier in the day that he might indeed help her with after all. She smiled wickedly. Two could play this little game of dangerous flirtation that he had started. She swallowed experimentally, and when she was certain she was able to communicate again, said, "Actually, you're right. There is something you can help me with."

He seemed surprised by her reply, but recovered himself quickly. Dropping his arms back to his sides, he replied, "Anything. Name it. I'll follow you anywhere."

"Would you mind following me upstairs, then?" she asked him as she stacked the last of Simon's sleepers onto the small pile. She lifted the clean laundry into her arms and approached Daniel slowly, meeting his gaze levelly as she neared. When she stood immediately before him, she paused, tilting her head back to smile up at him as suggestively as she could. "I need you for something upstairs," she said in a low whisper. "In my bedroom."

This time he didn't recover himself quite so quickly. A nerve jumped in his neck, and he cleared his throat awkwardly before saying roughly, "Oh?"

She nodded slowly, conspiratorially. "It's something I've been wanting you to do for me all day, ever since this afternoon, but... you know. You seemed so busy. And I didn't want to seem too forward."

He nodded, too, the action much faster and much less graceful than she had performed it herself. "I'm never too busy for you, Livy."

She patted his cheek affectionately. "Oh, it's so sweet of you to say that. Come on upstairs. First I want to put these things away in Simon's room and check to make sure he's still sleeping. I wouldn't want our... moving around so much... to wake him."

"No..." Daniel cleared his throat again. "Uh, no problem," he told her.

Olivia pushed past him and walked toward the stairs, trying to sway her hips back and forth seductively as she walked, hoping the motion didn't make her look as ridiculous as she felt. Simon was still sleeping soundly in his crib when she entered the nursery, so she tucked his things into a dresser drawer as quietly as she could and retreated to the hall. Daniel stood just beyond the doorway looking in, and she halted beside him to follow his gaze.

"I like how you fixed up the nursery," he whispered in deference to the sleeping child. She had rewound Simon's mobile before she left the room, and almost too slowly to see, the brightly colored elephant, giraffe, tiger and hippopotamus turned to a chirping tune. She watched Daniel survey the posters of jungle scenes, the lamp shaped like a lion, the scattering of toys. "Reminds me of an Amazon rain forest," he added.

Olivia nodded. "It turned out even better than I thought it would. It was nice being able to put Simon in this room. It used to be my room when I was a child. Mine and Sylvie's."

"This is the house you grew up in?" Daniel asked as he spun around to face her, clearly interested in her response. He seemed to have forgotten about the little tryst she was orchestrating. For now.

"From day one," she told him. "Like I said, Sylvie and I shared this room, and my older brother, Carver, was across the way, where my room is now. Mom and Dad had the big room downstairs, that's now the study."

Daniel nodded. "You know, I've heard you mention your brother before, but I don't recall ever meeting him."

Olivia smiled. "Carver is something of a gadabout. He does what he calls 'human interest stories' for *Left Bank* magazine."

"The magazine the GOP is suing for calling them...let's see if I remember the term correctly...'the fascist whored'?"

She winced, her expression a mixture of annoyance and pride. "Yeah, well, it *is* a liberal publication. In fact, I think Carver's the one who wrote the piece that coined the phrase. He doesn't spend much time in New Jersey—usually Sylvie and I will hear from him when he's passing through for a day or two. Otherwise..." she shrugged, "—we generally have no idea where he is at any given time." She glanced at the date on her watch. "Although he's due for an appearance anytime now. It's been almost a year since he was home. And he's anxious to meet his new nephew."

"It must be interesting living as an adult in the house where you grew up."

"Actually, it's kind of strange. When Mom died, I was living in a condo in Cherry Hill. Carver and Sylvie wanted to sell the house in Collingswood—they both have much more contemporary tastes, and thought the place was an eyesore—but I talked them out of it. I'm buying out their shares, slowly but surely. I like it here. I like it here a lot. It's a good neighborhood. A nice place for Simon to grow up, I think."

"So you grew up in Collingswood," Daniel said thoughtfully. "I grew up in Pennsauken. Here we were practically neighbors and never even knew it."

"How long did you live in Pennsauken?" Olivia asked, oddly delighted to discover this newfound tie between the two of them.

His lips tightened into a thin line, and he seemed reluctant to respond. Finally he said, "Until my eighteenth birthday. Then I left my parents' house without a backward glance, and never went back."

Something in his voice sobered Olivia immediately. He sounded almost angry all of a sudden. She knew she shouldn't pry, knew he'd volunteer any information he wanted her to have, but nevertheless she found herself asking, "Where did you go?"

"I moved into my own place," he said vaguely. "A friend of mine got me a job on a construction site that allowed me to support myself, and eventually I underwent carpenter's training." He was still gazing pensively at the sleeping baby when he continued. "My childhood wasn't a particularly happy one. Certainly not something I wanted to preserve any longer than I had to. Now, what's this thing you need me for in your bedroom?''

Daniel hated to cut the conversation short, especially in such an abrupt manner, and especially when Olivia was offering him snatches of her own background. But he had somehow found himself thrown into an area he had no desire to revisit, an area he wanted to avoid at all costs. Even at the risk of creating a rift between himself and Olivia.

But she didn't seem angry or hurt by his curt response, only confused and maybe a little sad. He found her reaction puzzling. Even he didn't feel sad anymore when he remembered the way he'd grown up. He'd gotten over all that years ago. And now that his old man was pushing up daisies, what was the point of dwelling on the past? The past was done and gone. It was time now to look toward the future. And for some reason, he found himself studying Olivia when he thought about that.

"In here," she said as she nodded toward her own room across the hall. She reached for the nursery door and closed it softly behind them.

When she turned around again, it was to find Daniel gazing at her with that lascivious look on his face again. "After you," he said, sweeping his arm toward her bedroom.

She smiled sweetly again, tempted to bat her eyelashes like an overanxious starlet, and made her way into her bedroom. "Over there," she said, pointing her finger in the general direction of the bed. Of course, on the other side of the bed was her closet, the part of her room to which she was actually pointing. But Daniel didn't have to know that. Not just yet.

"Over there?" he asked, his expression doubtful and hopeful at the same time. She fought back a smile, wishing more than anything that she could read his mind.

Olivia nodded. "Uh-huh. Is that a problem?"

"Uh, no. No. No problem at all."

She moved toward the bed, skimming her hand over the faded, hand-stitched quilt covering it as she passed by. She looked back over her shoulder flirtatiously. "I tried doing it by myself earlier," she said, "but I had trouble finding it. Then, when I finally did find it, I couldn't quite reach it. I even stood on a chair, thinking that might make it easier, but I *still* couldn't quite get at it. I thought you might have better luck with it, seeing as how your arms are much longer than mine."

When she turned around to face him more fully, she had to stifle her laughter, so panicked was the look on his face.

"Daniel?" she asked.

"Hmm?" The sound was startled, strangled and not a little confused.

"Could you help me reach it?"

He cleared his throat—something he seemed to be doing a lot lately—and eyed her suspiciously. "Tell me what *it* is exactly that you want me to reach for you."

"Oh, didn't I explain that part?"

"Well, I sort of thought you had—in your own way—but something tells me I might have been just a tad mistaken. *It* can be a lot of things, you know."

She slapped her open palm against her forehead and rolled her eyes toward the ceiling. "Oh, gee, didn't I tell you? I thought I'd told you. There's a big box of photographs up in the top of my closet that Sylvie wanted me to find for her. She's gotten it into her head that she wants to be the family historian. That's what I need you to reach."

She shook her head mildly before continuing, "Gosh, I bet you were thinking I meant something else, weren't you? You didn't realize I was pointing at the closet a minute ago, did you? You must have been thinking I was pointing at something else over here. Like the bed or something." She pretended to consider an idea that hadn't occurred to her before, widening her eyes in feigned shock. "Oh, no... You thought I *was* pointing at the bed, didn't you? That I was inviting you up here for a sexual encounter. Jeepers, Daniel, I'm so sorry I misled you that way. How silly of me. What you must be thinking of me right now I can only imagine."

Daniel crossed his arms over his chest and with a bored eye watched her overdramatize. When she finally concluded her monologue, he inhaled a deep sigh and released it slowly. "Are you finished?" he asked.

She pretended to consider the question for a moment before nodding.

"Okay, I guess I deserved that," he conceded. "I jumped to a conclusion, and it was quite obviously the wrong conclusion to make."

He crossed the bedroom with slow, deliberate strides, his movements reminding Olivia of one of those stealthy predators that showed up so frequently on the nature channel, the ones that seemed to be moving a lot more slowly than they actually were. As she watched him approach her, all her playfulness left her in a rush, replaced by a sexual awareness of the man stronger than any she had ever experienced before. Her body temperature seemed to soar to a feverish level, and the air around her seemed to burst into an incandescent heat.

For some reason, she suddenly wanted to lift a hand to cover herself, then reminded herself that nearly every inch of her body was covered beneath her neck. Something about Daniel's expression, though, made her feel as if she were completely naked. As he drew nearer, she instinctively began to back away from him. Unfortunately, her progress was halted almost immediately by the closet door behind her. So she only stood stiff, pressing herself flat against it, and watched him come closer.

He didn't pause until he stood within a scant inch of her. He didn't touch her, didn't move a single part of his body. But his gaze bored into hers and kept her bolted to the spot. She couldn't have fled if she'd wanted to. And deep down inside, Olivia knew fleeing Daniel was the last thing she wanted to do. Even if he did seem kind of angry about something.

"But if you lure me up into your bedroom again, Livy," he finally said, his voice so soft, she almost felt instead of heard the words, "be prepared for a different kind of conclusion. Because next time, I won't be so understanding. Next time, I'll definitely take you up on your offer."

She swallowed hard, wishing she could laugh off the tension that twisted inside her. However, when she tried to do just that, the only sound that emerged was a helpless little gurgle. When she finally found her voice again, it was to say softly, "I was only kidding, Daniel."

He settled one forearm against the closet door on each side of her face and leaned forward, then touched his lips to hers with one brief caress before pulling away. Just as she was beginning to enjoy it, she thought as disappointment wound through her.

His face still hovering over hers, he said quietly, "You may have been kidding, Livy, but I'm not." And with that he pushed himself away from her completely and straightened. "Now, where's this box of photos?" he asked as if nothing had happened.

Olivia slapped her hand hard against the closet door behind her, patting it a good three or four times more for emphasis. "Here," she said in a thin voice. "They're in here. Top shelf. Way up high."

Daniel cupped his hands over her shoulders, and for the briefest of moments, she was certain he was going to kiss her again. Almost of their own free will, her lips parted slightly, as if in preparation for the embrace. But instead of pressing his mouth against hers, he pushed her gently to the side and out of his way. Fighting down the feeling that she had been cheated, Olivia moved to stand behind him. Then he opened the closet door and searched the contents for the box in question. "Top shelf," she said again, hovering around him. "That big red box. See it?"

He reached up and plucked the big box easily from its resting place, then turned and dropped it unceremoniously onto the bed. "Anything else?" he asked impatiently.

She bit her lip thoughtfully. Actually, there had been something else she was going to ask him to do for her. But considering the frame of mind he was in now and the little scene the two of them had just shared, she wondered if now was an appropriate time to ask him for another favor. Oh, what the heck, she finally decided, throwing caution to the wind. The sooner she got started with this thing, the sooner she could get it over with.

"To be perfectly honest," she said, "yes. There is something else."

"Livy," he began, his voice laced with warning.

"No, not that," she was quick to add, lifting her hands palm up in front of her as if warding off a blow. "I'm not teasing this time. This is a legitimate favor—I promise."

He crossed his arms over his ample chest again, and as she noted once more the absolute exquisiteness and perfection of what lay beneath his shirt, she was reassured that he was exactly the right candidate for what she was about to ask him to do.

"What's the favor?" he asked, clearly still skeptical.

"I was wondering if you..." Her voice trailed off as she contemplated how best to put forth her question. Might as well just spit it out, she thought. "I was wondering if you might help me lose some weight."

Any flicker of hope that Daniel might have still entertained that Olivia was about to tumble him to the bed and have her way with him evaporated in a puff of mental steam. Losing weight. That was what she wanted him for. And as much as he wished her idea of burning up calories was the same as his own, he seriously doubted that sexual gymnastics was what she had in mind.

"Lose some weight," he repeated.

She nodded. "Well, you so much as offered your services this afternoon."

"I did?"

"Sure. You said you wouldn't mention my eating habits again unless I asked you about them. Well, now I'm asking you about them. I was also wondering if you might let me use some of the weight-lifting equipment in your basement and help me figure out how it all works."

Daniel lifted a hand to the back of his neck and rubbed at a tense knot that had risen up out of nowhere. Over the past two weeks, he had hoped that spending time with Olivia might open her eyes to the possibility of something more substantial than simple friendship between them. He had hoped she might come to see how much he needed her, and how much she needed him. However, he had also hoped that her need for him would be of the emotional, spiritual and sexual variety. He hadn't planned on her seeing him as a fitness requirement.

"It's just that I gained so much weight while I was pregnant with Simon," she began again, her voice pleading. "And none of my clothes fit anymore. I'm getting really sick of sweatpants and T- shirts. I can't even get into any of my nursing uniforms, and it's going to be so expensive to buy new ones."

When he still didn't reply, but continued to stare at her as if she were gradually fading out of sight, she continued, "I figure I've got more than two months before I have to go back to work. I could maybe lose fifteen or twenty pounds in that time, don't you think? At least I might be able to squeeze into something. Right?" When he still didn't respond, she prodded, "So do you think you could help me out?"

"I guess I could," he finally said, the statement surprising him. He wasn't certain just when he'd decided to speak, and he was quite sure he had intended to tell her he didn't have time to be her personal fitness trainer.

Because frankly, he didn't think it was such a good idea to spend any more time with Olivia than was absolutely necessary feeling the way he did about her. Perpetuating a physical closeness to her when an emotional one—at least to her way of thinking—was such an impossibility would probably bring him nothing but trouble. Still, it would give him an excuse to see her on a regular basis. That was better than nothing, right?

"You mean it?" Olivia asked. "Oh, Daniel, you're a lifesaver. I can't thank you enough." Without thinking, she stood on tiptoe and kissed him chastely on the cheek. When she realized what she had done, she quickly backed away. "I'm sorry," she said softly. "I didn't mean to—"

"Livy," he said quietly, lifting his hand to the cheek she had just kissed. "Don't . . ."

Don't what? she wondered. Don't apologize? Don't ever kiss him again? Don't ask for any more favors? He never finished the statement he had started to voice, and somehow Olivia got the feeling it was because he was no more certain of what he had intended to tell her than she was of what he was going to say. All that was important, she thought, was that Daniel would still be a part of her life, even when he'd finished the work on her house next week.

Then she quickly corrected herself. No, what was important was that soon she would be able to fit back into some of her clothes, she told herself emphatically. That was why she needed Daniel McGuane. He was helping her out the way any friend would. She'd be better off remembering that.

Six

"Okay, Simon, let's see what kind of stuff you're made of."

Daniel lifted the seven-week-old baby out of the bouncer and into his lap, tugging up one of the boy's tiny socks that had slipped down over his even tinier foot. He found himself baby-sitting again because Olivia had announced a need to run out to the grocery store just as he was sweeping up the last of the sawdust from the floor of her new back porch.

It had taken him a little longer to complete the work than he had originally anticipated, and he told himself that was because he had taken extra care to get the job done right, and not because he'd been trying to prolong his participation in Olivia's life. And his giddy delight at watching her son now, he thought further, came only from his desire to see more of the little guy, and not because Olivia lately seemed so willing to have Daniel spend time with him. He was, after all, sort of responsible for Simon, he thought. At least, for part of him.

Ever since a couple of weeks ago, when Olivia had asked him if he would play big brother, Daniel had been preoccupied with an odd sense of something it had taken him days to identify. He'd finally been able to nail it down as a sense of moral obligation. It was something he'd never experienced before, a reaction for which he'd been totally unprepared. Every morning for the past two weeks, he had come to the house next door with an exhilarated feeling of renewal, as if there were some newfound purpose in his life that made it more worth living. The little guy in his arms right now was the reason for that, he thought. And, he admitted reluctantly, so was the little guy's mother.

"Boy, you're getting heavy," he told the baby. "You must be topping the scales at ten pounds by now."

When Simon smiled at him, Daniel laughed. There was something strangely reassuring about being smiled at by a baby. It made him feel accepted in a way he never had before, made him feel as if he could do no wrong. He'd been told that at this age, babies generally only smiled because they had gas. But that wasn't true of Simon. Oh, no. Not only was this baby cuter, quicker and more responsive than the average baby, this baby was also smarter. If Simon was smiling, it was because there was a very good reason to smile.

"So what's on the agenda for the afternoon?" he asked the infant. "Let's see, what have you done so far today? You woke up—that was a good way to start the morning. Then you ate—something else that gets the day rolling along smoothly—and then, according to your mother, you filled your diaper really well. All in all, I'd say you've just about covered the scope of a baby's curriculum vitae."

Simon smiled again, and Daniel laughed harder. "So what else is there, hmm? Let's see now, there must be something Uncle Daniel could show you or tell you that you haven't seen or heard about yet." He paused thoughtfully, then added, "Well, actually, there's a lot Uncle Daniel could show you and tell you about that you haven't seen or heard yet, but your mom would skin me alive if I exposed you to any of that stuff before your eighteenth birthday, so..."

He thought for a moment longer, staring through the screen out at the backyard. The June temperature hovered just below eighty, and the sun hung high in a pale blue sky. A soft breeze trembled through the trees, making them beckon to him with a whisper and a wave.

"Hey," he said to Simon, "have you had a nature walk yet?" When the baby stared back at him with a blank expression, Daniel figured he had his answer. "No, I don't think you have. And that's something every baby needs to take while he's still young and impressionable enough to enjoy it."

He tucked his hands under Simon's arms and lifted him so that the infant's face was level with his own. "What do you say, pal? It's a nice day. Your mom has a great garden back there. What say we go check it out?"

Simon kicked his legs enthusiastically and made a little noise, one that Daniel was certain meant he was eager to get out of the house for a while. Together, they foraged around the house until they located Simon's diaper bag, where Daniel located a pair of minuscule Wayfarer sunglasses and the smallest Phillies baseball cap he had ever seen in his life. He chuckled at the sight of the miniature sports fan when he got the baby dressed; then together they ventured outdoors.

The sun was warm on Daniel's face, and Simon turned his head immediately away from the bright light. He hoisted the baby against his shoulder and away from the sunlight and placed his open palm over Simon's back, marveling yet again at just how small and fragile the infant was. He himself had been about that size at one time, he thought, amazed to think that something twenty-three inches long and weighing ten pounds could potentially put on more than four feet and two hundred pounds before his growing was done.

"You'll get there," he told Simon. "You've got a few decades to do it, but you'll get there." And what was the rush, anyway? he wondered. There was plenty to keep the little guy occupied between now and manhood.

Daniel stepped into the shade and turned Simon to face him again, pulling down the leafy branch of a sugar maple to brush a leaf against the baby's face. Simon lifted a hand toward the limb, following closely the motion of the leaf with his eyes. Then, very slowly and with much deliberation, he reached up and grabbed the leaf, latching on with his tiny fist and not letting go.

"Hey, Simon," Daniel said with a chuckle. "Way to go." Although he'd noticed the baby reaching toward things in the past weeks, he'd never seen him follow through with a grip on something. This was a milestone, he thought. Olivia was going to be so excited.

He looked back toward the house then, and, as if conjured by his thoughts, the woman in question stood just outside the back door watching him with the baby. The sunlight danced with the breeze in her hair, lighting flickering, golden fires in the dark, tousled curls. Her red cotton tank dress hugged her body with much affection, displaying an abundance of curves and slopes that he found bewitching.

In two weeks of dieting and working out, she'd dropped three pounds, but to Daniel, the loss was immaterial. Olivia Venner was a beautiful woman, regardless of her weight, her height, her hair color, her eyes, her style. He wasn't sure what it was that made her so stunning, but there was something there that he simply couldn't resist, and for the life of him, he wished he knew what to do about that.

She was watching him and Simon closely and seemed to be thinking hard about something, so intent was her gaze. For a long moment, Daniel could only stare back at her. Finally he was startled out of his reverie by the squirming bundle in his arms. When he looked down at Simon, the baby's eyes were hidden by the dark glasses, but he could have sworn the little guy was studying him as closely as his mother seemed to be. It was a disconcerting feeling, one he wasn't sure how to interpret.

Olivia, too, was feeling more than a little discomposed as she watched her next-door neighbor cradling her son. When she'd come home from the grocery store to discover the house empty, she had immediately gone to the back door. And when she'd seen Daniel walking with Simon beneath the big maple tree, the strangest thing had happened.

For the most fleeting of moments, she had been impressed by weirdest sensation. As she had watched the two of them together, had observed Daniel's gentleness with the baby and Simon's ready response to the big man, she had almost felt as if the two of them were father and son.

There was no reason for the feeling, really, she thought, but there it was just the same. What was truly astounding, though, was that the feeling hadn't shocked her, hadn't come as a surprise at all. There was something about the idea that simply felt...*right*. Something inside of her that told her Daniel should have been the man to father Simon.

But that was ridiculous, she tried to tell herself further. Because Daniel was her friend, not her lover. And she had no intention of ever changing that.

Although Olivia had long ago conceded that her next-door neighbor was an attractive enough man, she had never considered him to be sexy. Not until he'd invaded her house to rebuild a part of it. Not until she'd started seeing him on a daily basis, shared lunch and conversation with him, noticed how gentle he was with her son. Not until that heated kiss the two of them had shared in her kitchen two weeks ago. After that, of course, she hadn't been able to help but notice.

But Daniel was so *nice,* she thought. So kind and so...so...*decent.* And she'd simply never had a thing for nice, decent guys. It would never work out between her and Daniel. She'd always liked men who were takers, men who led dangerous lives and had no concern for much of anything. Hazardous men. Exciting men. Men who provided a woman with a real challenge—even if that challenge was something she was seldom able to overcome. And Daniel McGuane simply didn't fit that bill at all.

But the reassurances did nothing to soothe Olivia's frazzled thoughts. When she looked at Daniel and Simon, she still saw two guys who seemed to belong together. Two guys who could smile at her and change the way she felt about everything. Two guys who confounded and confused the heck out of her.

Pushing her troubling contemplations away for the time being, she strode across the backyard to where those two guys still stood staring back at her. She smiled at the picture Simon made in his sunglasses and baseball cap, then bent forward to kiss his warm cheek. As she pulled away from the baby, she experienced the strange desire to perform the same gesture with Daniel. Only, her kiss for him would land somewhere besides his cheek, she thought idly, and would be anything but motherly in intent.

"Was he a good boy while I was gone?" she asked, brushing Simon's nose playfully with her finger.

"Are you talking to him or me?" Daniel asked.

She smiled. "I'll let you answer first. Simon and I can talk later."

"He was a very good boy," he assured her.

"Good."

"And," he added proudly, "watch what he can do."

He reached up for the tree branch again and pulled it down toward the baby, dangling a bright green leaf just within Simon's reach. Once again, the infant followed the leaf's movement intently with his gaze, then, as slowly and deliberately as before, he reached out a hand and grabbed it, trying to pull it toward him.

"He caught it," Olivia cried, delighted. "He can hold things now."

Daniel nodded. "He did it a couple of minutes ago for the first time."

Her face fell, disappointment etched on her features. "Oh, no, and I wasn't here to see it. A major first for my son, and I missed it."

Daniel looked abashed. "I'm sorry, I shouldn't have said anything. I wasn't thinking. I should have let you discover this by yourself. I—"

Immediately, Olivia's expression cleared, and she smiled. "No, that's okay," she told him, lifting a hand to his shoulder to reassure him. "Maybe I wasn't here, but you were. You were here to share this with Simon." She shrugged, honestly happy about the event. "And that makes it all right."

Daniel smiled back. "Thanks, Livy."

She shook her head. "No. Thank *you*."

"For what?"

"For being there for Simon. Now and in the future. I really do appreciate it."

He surveyed her without expression. "I'm here for you, too, you know. Whenever you need me. Whatever you need me for."

She looked away, watching the maple leaves shiver against the warm summer wind. "I know," she said softly. "And I appreciate that, too."

"I just wanted to make sure that was clear."

She nodded, but continued to focus her gaze somewhere other than his face. "So what are your plans for the evening? You want to join me and Simon for dinner?"

"What are you having?"

"Well, I wanted to fix lasagna with extra cheese and a brie salad and butter pecan ice cream for dessert—"

"Livy..." he cautioned.

She wrinkled her nose in disgust. "—but instead I'm going to grill some chicken breasts, make some brown rice and steam some carrots, broccoli and cauliflower with a little dill and lemon juice."

"Good girl," he said with a smile. "We'll turn you into a good eater yet."

"Oh, I'm a *great* eater," she told him. "Unfortunately, I just hate all this stuff you've got me fixing."

"You'll get used to it," he promised her.

"Don't count on it. So you staying for dinner or not?"

"I'd love to."

"Good."

Simon yawned widely then, signaling his satisfaction with the day's botany lesson and his desire that it be ended for now. Olivia took him from Daniel's arms, and when the baby rooted around her breast, decided it would be best to feed her son before fixing dinner for herself and Daniel.

The thought was comforting, one that made her feel content. A full, sleeping baby upstairs while she and Daniel shared a meal together downstairs. It was an image she wanted to hold in her mind for a long time, but one she knew she should find incongruent. Because Daniel simply wasn't the kind of man she wanted in her life. He would be great for Simon, certainly, but he wasn't the man for her.

Someday he'd be a wonderful husband and father to someone, she realized. But instead of being warmed by the thought, Olivia suddenly felt chilled. Because when that day came, Daniel would have less and less reason to be a part of her life with Simon. Gradually, he might even disappear for good.

And that, she decided, just didn't seem right at all.

Maybe this wasn't such a good idea after all.

Olivia broke the nine-word thought into four relatively equal installments to help her count every time she pushed the thirty-pound barbell over her head. There was a word for the way she felt about working out, but she was too nice a girl to put voice or thought to it. So instead, she just focused on what had lately become her mantra.

Maybe this... wasn't such... a good idea... after all. Release. She inhaled deeply and gripped the bar again, shoving the weight upward and away from her prone body for the eighteenth time. Perspiration trickled from her forehead in thin streams to her hair, winding slowly through the damp tresses toward the back of her neck, then lingering there in a warm pool. She inhaled deeply before pushing the barbell upward and away from her again. *This definitely... wasn't such... a good idea... after all.* Release.

As she tried to regulate her breathing, she turned her head to look toward the other side of Daniel's basement. There, sitting in some weird contraption, the top half of which reminded her of a huge, padded butterfly, she saw the man she had so foolishly asked to help her lose weight.

Ha, she thought now. She'd barely lost five pounds since the two of them had started working out together a month ago. Daniel had tried to assure her that it was because she was building up heavier weight in her muscles while losing the lighter-weight fat she so despised, something to be expected when working out with weights. And she had gone down a dress size, she recalled grudgingly. Even Sylvie had helped out, coming to her rescue with the loan of some of her nicer outfits, so at least Olivia didn't have to rely on her hated maternity clothes and sweats any longer.

Nevertheless, she was still topping the scales at a much higher number than she wanted to, and with her return to work only a few weeks away, she still couldn't get her uniforms buttoned.

"How's it going over there?" Daniel called out to her when he looked up to find her watching him. "Did you finish your twenty-five rotations?"

"Yes," she lied. Then, lowering her voice to a whisper, she added, "All but seven of them."

"What?" he asked.

"Nothing."

"You know, it's funny, but from over here, I'd swear it looked like you only did eighteen rotations."

She narrowed her eyes anxiously. "Really? Only eighteen?"

"Mmm, hmm."

She swiped at the beads of perspiration dotting her upper lip. "Gee, that is funny, isn't it? You must have some strange, other-dimensional time warp in your basement that makes things seem to go more slowly than they actually do. We should call 'Unsolved Mysteries' about it."

He smiled. "Or maybe it's just that you miscounted."

Yep, that was Daniel, Olivia thought with a sigh. Too polite to accuse her of lying, even when it was obvious that she had been. He would always be a gentleman until the end.

"So you think it was only eighteen, huh?" she asked, curling her fingers once again around the heavy metal bar that lay ten inches above her head.

He nodded. "Of course, it could be that *I'm* the one who's mistaken."

She wanted to stick her tongue out at him, but caught herself just before completing the action. "No, no, I'll take your word for it," she said magnanimously. "I did have my mind on other things while I was counting. Could be that I missed a rotation or two." Or seven, she concluded to herself.

Daniel went back to pumping the wings of the big metal butterfly in and out with what seemed to be almost no effort, and Olivia stifled a groan. She hadn't been lying when she'd told him she'd had her mind on other things while she was working out. What she had neglected to elaborate on, however, was that every single one of those "other things" involved Daniel McGuane. Or, more specifically, Daniel McGuane's body. Particularly the way it looked all sheened with sweat and straining against the machines designed to sculpt it even more.

Lifting the weight high above her once again, she turned her head to sneak another peek at him. As he always did when the two of them worked out together, he wore nothing but a pair of brief, gray sweatpants tied in a loose knot just below his waist. His sandy hair hung in lank, damp strands over his forehead, and thin rivulets of sweat rolled and twisted down his abdomen to darken the waistband all the way around. The muscles in his forearms bulged until thick veins threaded through the sinew, and she could almost swear she saw his life's blood pulsing there. His torso, too, was alive with activity, muscles she'd only seen before in her anatomy textbooks dancing to life with every movement he made.

It wasn't fair, she thought. It wasn't fair that a man who was destined to be nothing more than her good buddy had a body she'd drool over for the rest of her life.

She finished up her seven rotations, then lay still and stared at the ceiling. Simon was next door with Zoey, who had stopped by to see the baby on her way home from work and fill Olivia in on the latest gossip about the goings-on in the Seton General maternity ward. Zoey had also—rather enthusiastically, she recalled now—volunteered to baby-sit when Olivia had announced her need to go next door for her workout with Daniel. That had been almost an hour ago, and she knew she shouldn't infringe on Zoey's time any more than she had to.

"I think I'm just going to do my cool-down and head out," she said. "Zoey probably needs to get home."

"Oh, I forgot to tell you," Daniel said as he, too, finished up his own activity. "She called just before you got over here and said she was going to take Simon out for a little fresh air. She told me to tell you she had packed the bottle of milk you expressed earlier that was in the fridge, along with some spare diapers and other stuff, but that she would have the baby home before dark." He shrugged, the gesture seeming a little self-conscious to Olivia. "She said she thought you needed a few hours to yourself," he concluded.

Olivia cupped a palm over her forehead and sighed. No, she mused, what Zoey thought she needed was a few hours alone with Daniel.

"And since you've cooked dinner for me so often over the past couple of months," he went on, "I thought maybe I could return the favor and make dinner for you tonight."

"It's sweet of you to offer," Olivia told him as she jack-knifed into a sitting position and swiped a hand across the back of her damp neck. Deep down, she wanted more than anything to take him up on his suggestion. But given the waywardness of her thoughts about Daniel lately, she also knew it would probably be wiser not to. "And thanks, but it's really not necessary. I cooked for you because you were helping me out." She indicated the weight settled in its holder beside her. "You're still helping me out. So you don't owe me anything."

He reached for a towel and wiped his face and chest, his hands making slow, circular motions as they moved downward. Olivia found the action fascinating, and her gaze never left him as he performed it.

"Then let me make dinner for you because I want to," he told her.

She opened her mouth to tell him no, but instead heard herself say, "Okay."

She arrowed her eyebrows down in confusion as she contemplated the unexpectedness of her reply, but Daniel's obvious delight in her answer prevented her from too much consideration. Because as pleased as he looked that she had agreed to stay and have dinner with him, she knew that she was doubly pleased to be doing it. And that confused her even more.

"I'll jump in the shower first, if that's okay," he said. "Then I'll get to work on dinner while you clean up."

She nodded, an odd thrill of excitement winding through her at the thought of using Daniel's shower so soon after he'd used it himself. Then she realized that it would of course be far more practical for her to run next door and shower at her own house. Not only would she be surrounded by all of her own toiletries, but she could change her clothes, as well.

"I can shower at home," she said, hoping the disappointment she felt didn't find its way into her voice. "That way I can put on some clean clothes, too."

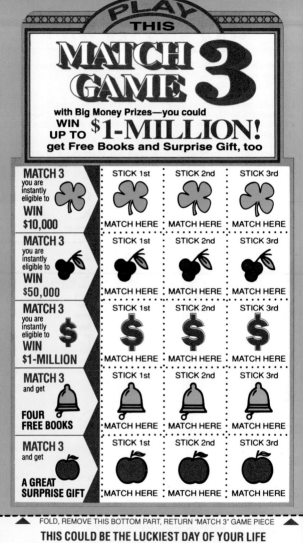

Use These Stamps to Complete Your
"MATCH 3" Game

Simply detach this page & see how many matches you can find for your "MATCH 3" Game. Then take the matching stamps and stick them on the Game. Three-of-a-kind matches in rows 1 through 3 qualify you for a chance to win a Big Money Prize—up to a Million-$$$ ...

... THREE-OF-A-KIND-MATCHES IN ROWS 4 & 5 GETS YOU FREE BOOKS & A NICE SURPRISE GIFT AS WELL! PLAYING IS FREE - FUN - EASY & THE WAY YOU COULD WIN! *PLAY TODAY!*

PLAY "MATCH 3"—YOU COULD WIN UP TO
A MILLION-$$$ IN LIFETIME INCOME (YES, $1,000,000!)
—GET FREE BOOKS & AN EXCITING SURPRISE GIFT, TOO!

★ Did you complete the first 3 rows of your "Match 3" Game? Did you print your name & address on the Game? Are you also playing & enclosing your Bonus Games? Please do, because so doing definitely qualifies you for a chance to win one of the Fabulous Prizes being offered, up to & including a MILLION-$$$ in Lifetime Income!

★ Did you complete rows 4 & 5? If you did, you are entitled to Free Books & a really nice Surprise Gift, as your introduction to our Reader Service. The Service does not require you to buy, ever. When you get your Free Books, if you don't want any more, just write cancel on the statement & return it to us.

★ You can of course go for prizes alone by not playing rows 4 & 5. But why pass up such good things? Why not go for all the prizes you can - & why not get everything that's being offered & that you're entitled to? It's all free, yours to keep & enjoy. It's a "SURE FIRE" opportunity for you!

His expression was sheepish. "Ah, yeah, I guess that does make more sense, doesn't it?"

The temperature in the cool basement seemed to be rising fast to a boiling point, so Olivia quickly stood and reached for her own towel. She draped it over her shoulders and spent an inordinate amount of time wiping the perspiration from her face, knowing the heated flush that had crept over her skin was less the result of an extensive workout than it was the result of the thoughts parading through her brain. Thoughts about being naked in Daniel's shower. Thoughts about being naked in Daniel's shower with Daniel. Thoughts about being naked in Daniel's shower with Daniel while the two of them were—

"I won't be long," she mumbled from behind the white terry cloth as she hurried toward the basement steps. "No more than half an hour."

She nearly tripped up the steps, so hastily did she beat her retreat. She didn't stop running until she was safely ensconced in her bedroom at home. By that time, her breathing was coming in rapid gasps, and her blood was rushing through her veins with a speed that might just qualify her for the Kentucky Derby. And Olivia knew full well that such a reaction had nothing at all to do with an afternoon of exercise, nor was it a result of her hurried flight from next door.

Seven

Her first taste of wine since discovering she was pregnant so many months ago had been delicious, Olivia thought with a satisfied sigh as she sipped a little more from her second glass. And what Daniel had served with dinner was much better than the screw-top variety she had always imbibed before. She should have known that Daniel McGuane—although conscientious about his health—would at least indulge occasionally, and that when he did, he would only drink the finest. In addition to his weights in the basement, she had noticed a modest collection of wine, and it had been from that "wine cellar" in the corner of the room that he had selected this.

Yes, it was delicious, she thought as she sipped slowly again. Every bit as delicious as dinner had been, maybe even more so. She knew she probably should have stopped at one glass—Simon would no doubt later voice his displeasure at her self-indulgence—but she couldn't remember the last time she had shared a table with a man without having to worry about the repercussions of her actions. And for the first time in a long time, she had done something just for herself.

Instead of her usual sweats and T-shirt, she had dressed in a sleeveless, button-front white cotton sheath that she had on loan from Sylvie. For the first time since Simon's birth, she had applied a little makeup to her face, had slipped long, dangly earrings through her earlobes and fastened a thin, gold chain around her neck. She had even dabbed on a little perfume in all the intimate places a woman normally wore it. And all the while she had told herself that she was doing these things only because she was finally feeling better about herself. And she almost, *almost*, even believed that all the primping was in fact for herself alone.

Tonight, for the first time in months, Olivia had let herself completely and utterly relax. And tonight, for the first time in months, she had enjoyed herself immeasurably.

Now she sat at a card table in Daniel's dining room, reveling in the sweet aroma of sawdust that seemed to permeate his entire house, watching the way the stubby candle at the table's center spilled ethereal light and ghostly shadows over the room. As she listened to the sounds he made while cleaning up in the kitchen, she marveled again at what a good cook he was. Why, he'd actually made healthy food seem tasty. Maybe when she was done with her weight training, she could ask him if he was interested in offering cooking classes. She had never had squash prepared quite that way before.

With another contented sigh, she blew out the candle and drained the rest of her glass, then carried it into the kitchen. Daniel was loading the last of the pots and pans into the dishwasher, and she paused in the doorway to admire the way his faded jeans hugged his lower extremes with much familiarity. His white T-shirt, too, displayed the solid expanse of his back with exquisite accuracy, and she wished she were the one who surrounded him so completely.

When she came up behind him to set her wineglass on the counter, she placed her open palm on his back to let him know she was behind him. Immediately, she felt the muscles beneath her fingers tighten fiercely; then he straightened and spun around.

"My glass," she said softly, surprised by his reaction. "I was just going to set it by the sink, and I didn't want to startle you when I did."

She hadn't moved her hand when he had pivoted to face her, and now her splayed fingers lay open against his rigid abdomen. For one luxurious moment, Olivia allowed herself the indulgence of touching him, soaking in his warmth and strength before she forced herself to curl her hand into a loose fist against him. Yet still she did not—could not—remove her hand completely.

"You didn't startle me," he told her, closing his own fist over hers. With his free hand, he plucked the wineglass from her grasp and set it gently on the counter beside him. "At least, not the way you think you did."

She stared at the wet, soapy fingers curved over her own, at the obvious differences between them. Daniel's hand was twice the size of Olivia's, burnished a dark bronze over the ridges of tendons and blood vessels where hers was a pale ivory that clearly displayed the blue veins beneath her skin.

He could probably crush every delicate bone in her hand with one squeeze if he wanted to, she thought. And she knew that although such a realization would make some men feel more powerful, she was certain it was something that would never even occur to Daniel. It was his obvious strength mixed with his undeniable gentleness that so fascinated her. Here was a man who should be a swaggering, arrogant egomaniac, yet he was more human than anyone she had ever met. He was an enigma. And Olivia found herself wanting more than anything to unravel him.

"But you do startle me, Livy," he said, bringing her thoughts back to the tension that had been tightening the air between them for weeks. His voice was low, level and very, very serious.

"I do?" she asked, feeling suddenly breathless. Her gaze wandered upward, from their entangled fingers to his face, a face that was at once peaceful and turbulent, satisfied and yearning. Without even thinking about what she was doing, she lifted her free hand to his cheek, and threaded her fingers through his hair. "In what way do I...startle you?"

He mimicked her action, settling his own hand over the slender column of her throat and brushing his thumb over her jaw. She felt as if a white-hot serpent was coiled within her, ready to strike spitting flames. The sensation of Daniel's warm, rough hand against her already heated flesh made her feel as if she were about to be consumed by fire. His fire. Her eyelids fluttered closed as she tried to steady herself.

"I think you know in what way," he told her.

Olivia started to shake her head in denial, but he halted the action by moving his other hand to her cheek. She opened her eyes to find her face cradled in his warm palms, and Daniel gazing at her intently, contemplating her as if she, too, were a puzzle he had long sought to solve.

"You startled me the very first day I saw you," he told her.

She felt as if someone had dunked her into a hot pool—her head was swimming, she felt utterly weightless and everything suddenly seemed so quiet. "I did?"

He nodded. "And it's only gotten worse over the past two years."

"It has?"

Instead of answering her verbally, Daniel bent his head and brushed his lips softly against hers. When he pulled away, Olivia had closed her eyes again, but her lips were still slightly pursed, as if she were waiting for him to kiss her again. And as much as he wanted to accommodate her silent request, he checked himself, waiting for her to make the next move.

Finally she opened her eyes—those dark eyes the color of rich coffee, eyes whose compelling combination of earnestness and passion had often kept him awake for hours at night—and Daniel felt himself drowning. She studied him for a long time, as if she were trying as hard as he to understand what had suddenly changed between them. And then, without even thinking about what she was doing, she raised herself up on tiptoe to press her lips to his cheek.

When she pulled away, she asked, "You aren't the kind of man who would get a woman drunk and then take advantage of her, are you, Daniel?"

He shook his head. "No, I'm not. Why? Are you drunk?"

She sighed, a longing sound, and shook her head as well. "Not even the slightest bit tipsy."

"Then I don't guess I'm taking advantage of you, am I?"

"Not yet, no." She smiled in invitation, then curled her arm around his neck and pulled his face toward hers. "But I wish you'd hurry up and get on with it."

It was all the encouragement he needed. Pressing his lips to hers, he took her mouth with all the pent-up desire he had suppressed for weeks, even years. Kissing Olivia was something he had dreamed about on hundreds of occasions, and the single embrace they'd shared two weeks ago had only fueled his desire—his *need*—to know more. He buried his fist in her hair, coiling a few thick strands tightly around his fingers, then dropped his other hand to the small of her back, urging her body closer to his. He was vaguely aware of her wrapping her arm around his waist, and then he lost himself to her.

She smelled wonderful. Like some wicked Orient breeze hurtling across a vast ocean. She was warm where he touched her, softer than he could have imagined, and she seemed to surround him completely. As he kissed her more deeply, all he could think about was how much more of her he wanted. Turning his body so that he was leaning against the counter, he dropped his hand to her hip and pressed her insistently into the most intimate part of himself.

Olivia groaned at the feel of Daniel's body so entwined with her own. Her fingers explored every inch of him she could reach, only to discover that he was hot and hard everywhere she touched him. She gasped when the fingers twisting in her hair tightened, and instinctively she opened up to him more fully. As he plundered her mouth, she turned on him, taking her own liberties in tasting him as deeply. But when his other hand dropped to her hip, when he pushed her more completely against himself and she felt how quickly and completely he had responded to their embrace, she was helpless to keep herself from going limp.

Daniel took advantage of her momentary retreat by pivoting their bodies around so that Olivia was the one pressed against the counter. With one final, lengthy kiss, he easily lifted her off the ground, until she was seated on the counter before him. Their hold on each other thus somewhat relieved, he looked at her with longing, his face flushed with the heat of his desire, his breathing coming in rapid, ragged rasps.

For a long time they only stared at each other; then Daniel lifted a hand to the top button of her dress. He brushed his index finger back and forth across it thoughtfully, although his eyes never left hers, then slipped the button carefully through its hole. When Olivia settled her hands on his shoulders and offered no indication that she wanted him to stop, he dropped his hand to the second button and slowly, oh so slowly, freed it, too.

Without looking away from her face, and with leisurely movements that nearly drove her mad, he performed the same function for the next several buttons, until her dress opened slightly to her waist. She felt his warm breath condense on the heated flesh between her breasts, and her fingers flexed, tightening their hold on his shoulders. He must have interpreted her action as an invitation—which, she supposed, she had intended it to be—because he leaned forward and placed his mouth over the skin he had just warmed.

Olivia moaned out loud at the feel of him kissing her so intimately. He lifted a hand to push aside the fabric of her dress, then curved his fingers gently over the swell of her breast, rubbing his thumb rhythmically over the already rigid peak. When she groaned again, he nipped her playfully with his teeth, then laved his tongue over the spot with great care. A shiver wound through her body, a combination of heat and cold like nothing she'd ever experienced before. Twisting her fingers in his hair, she pulled his head away from her and bent to kiss him, a kiss more complete than any she had ever given.

It was a kiss that nearly consumed him. As Olivia plundered his mouth with hers, Daniel reached for her, pulling her off the counter and into his arms. When she wound her legs around his waist, he easily held her aloft. Then, as if lost in a somnambulistic daze, he carried her from the kitchen toward the stairs without interrupting their embrace. There, he settled her on the steps while he remained on the floor, a posture that made her height slightly more equal to his. He continued to kiss her, freely exploring her back and shoulders as he did so, then halted his explorations as abruptly as they had begun.

Somehow, Daniel forced himself to pull away from Olivia, but only far enough to gauge her reactions to what he intended to say to her. The sight of her nearly undid him, however, and his words caught temporarily in his throat. She looked rumpled and wind-tossed, thanks to his very physical attentions, her cheeks pink, her eyes nearly black with wanting. In the pale glow of the setting sun that fell in shafts of amber and gold through the dining room windows, she seemed almost otherworldly, and he still couldn't quite convince himself that what was happening between them was truly real.

"I'm going to make love to you, Livy," he said, somehow managing to keep his voice level in spite of the turmoil churning around inside him. "Unless you stop me right this instant, I'm going to take you upstairs to my bed, strip every inch of clothing from your body and make love to you until we're both too weak to do anything but lie in each other's arms wanting more."

A shock of electricity shot through her at the fierceness of his vow, and she gripped his shoulders tightly lest she dissolve in a heap of fallen womanhood at his feet. "I know," she told him. "It's something that's been coming for a long time, I think. Something I don't think either one of us could stop if we wanted to."

There was a slight edge to her statement that bothered him, but he was too preoccupied with other, more urgent, needs to give it the full consideration it warranted. "Do you want to stop?" he asked instead.

She shook her head. "No. Do you?"

"No way."

She lifted her hand to the hair that had fallen over his forehead and brushed it back gently, her fingers lingering in the soft tresses. "Then don't stop. By all means, continue with what we started. Make love to me, Daniel. Make love to me now."

He had to fight off his body's insistence that he follow her instructions to the letter and hike up her skirt to take her right there on the stairs. Lifting her into his arms again with much more aplomb than he had managed the first time, he effortlessly carried her up the stairs. In his bedroom, he lay her carefully down on his bed. Because the east-facing room was sheltered by an expansive tree outside, it was denied the soft radiance of the setting sun. He reached for the lamp on the bedside table, but his motion was halted by Olivia's voice, a voice that sounded almost tremulous and uncertain.

"No," she said, circling his wrist with insistent fingers. "Don't turn on the light."

"But I want to see you. I want—"

"In the dark, Daniel, please."

"But why?"

The little light that did manage to penetrate the bedroom mingled with the yellow glow of an early-burning street lamp outside, gilding her in a soft aura. It was enough illumination for him to see her shrug, but her face was in shadow, and he wasn't quite able to decipher her expression.

"I don't know," she said. "It just seems more natural this way, that's all."

He thought her statement puzzling, but didn't press the issue. Instead he reached behind himself to grab a fistful of his T-shirt in his hand, pulled the soft cotton over his head to toss it in a heap on the floor, then moved to join her on the bed. She lay on her side facing him, and immediately her hands went to his naked chest.

"You are so beautiful," she told him, tracing her finger along the well-defined lines of his musculature. "I don't think I've ever seen a more beautiful man than you."

He chuckled, a low, deeply sexual sound. "And although I've been called a lot of things in my life—most of them not polite enough for repeating—I don't think anyone's ever called me 'beautiful' before."

Olivia sighed as she dipped her fingers lower, following the ridges of his hard belly. "Then you've been hanging around with a bunch of silly, sightless people," she told him.

His hand closed over hers and halted her journey just as she found her way to the waistband of his jeans. "Lately, you're the only one I've been hanging around with, Livy."

She didn't reply to his statement, but he could see her turn her face toward his in the darkness. He lifted a hand to the buttons still fastened on her dress and slowly unhooked each of them until the pale fabric lay completely open. Beneath her dress, she wore only a lacy brassiere and panties. Daniel touched his index finger to the hollow at her throat and lazily skimmed it downward, pausing at the front closure of her bra before dipping down to circle her navel and venture onward to the waistband of her panties. Then he dared to move lower still, cupping his hand over the most intimate part of her. His breathing became shallow when he felt how warm and anxious she was for him already. Brushing his hand upward again, he shoved one side of her dress away and over her shoulder.

"You're the one who's beautiful," he said in a reverent whisper. "Everything about you is..."

When his voice trailed off without completing the statement, Olivia quietly urged him, "What? What about me, Daniel?"

He shook his head as he searched for the appropriate words. "I don't know," he finally replied honestly. "You're everything I've ever imagined a woman could be, and more. You're not like anyone else I've ever known. You're...you feel so...so *right*, Livy. Does that make sense at all?"

She didn't reply in the affirmative or negative, only continued to watch him silently. Then, when he thought her lack of response would drive him crazy, she rose up into a sitting position, shed her dress and lay back down again. Then she reached for his hand and guided it back to the soft spot above her thighs he had touched so intimately before, and leaned forward to kiss him.

Daniel stroked her deeply over the damp cotton covering her as he kissed her back, touching his other hand to the clasp of her bra and levering his finger beneath it before freeing the garment and pushing it away. She felt glorious beneath, her skin a combination of silk and fire, of purity and passion. Her heartbeat beneath his fingertips was wild and erratic, completely uncontrolled, as he was himself. He rolled over and brought Olivia with him, spreading his fingers open over her bare back, and reveling in the weight of her atop him.

The touch of Daniel's naked flesh against her own sent Olivia's senses spiraling in a flash of frenzy. When she tried to push herself up and away from him, he wrapped his arms around her waist and held her firmly in place, lifting his head to her breasts, kissing each one with infinite care. As he dragged his tongue over the lower swell of one breast, his hands dipped beneath the fabric of her panties, spreading open over her derriere, pushing her down toward him, forcing her to feel how much he needed and wanted her.

"Oh," she whispered when she felt the heavy proof of his desire. "Oh, Daniel."

He rolled over again, until she lay beneath him, and rubbed himself languorously against her, back and forth and back again, like a cat who took its time stretching. Then, without warning, he moved away from her.

"Daniel?" she asked. "What's wrong? Where are you going?"

Olivia watched as his hand rose to the first button on his jeans, and understanding dawned on her. With as much care as he had shown unbuttoning her, Daniel unbuttoned himself, shedding the remainder of his clothing to stand before her, gloriously naked. For a moment, she regretted her suggestion that he not turn on a light. Then he turned so that the lamplight filtering through the blinds caressed him like a lover, and she caught her breath at the magnificence of his form.

"Did I say you were beautiful just a minute ago?" she asked quietly. "I daresay I spoke too soon." She shook her head slowly in wonder, contemplating him more completely. "You're much more than beautiful, Daniel. I'm not sure there is a word to adequately describe what you are."

"Hungry," he told her instantly. "That's exactly what I am. Hungry for something only you can give me."

"Then come back to bed," she said with a heartfelt sigh. "And I'll do my best to satisfy you."

He didn't immediately respond as she had requested, but he moved slowly toward her. "Are you taking any precautions right now?" he asked.

She looked at him, puzzled. "What do you mean?"

"I mean are you taking anything to keep from getting pregnant?"

"Well, I'm still nursing Simon," she said. "That's supposed to prevent me from conceiving."

"Is that a guarantee?"

She shrugged. "To be perfectly honest, I don't know."

He stood for a moment, seeming to think about something, then turned and went to a dresser on the other side of the room. When he returned he was holding something Olivia recognized right away, something wrapped tightly in a flat, shiny, perfectly square package, something she probably should have been carrying with her herself the night that Simon was conceived.

"I won't do to you what Steve did," Daniel told her. "I won't make you pregnant and then abandon you."

She pressed her lips tightly together to keep silent the conflux of emotions that spun through her at his roughly uttered declaration. "Thanks," she said. "You're a good guy, Daniel."

Daniel bit back the sardonic laughter that threatened to erupt inside him. A good guy? he thought. Oh, sure. That could be the only reason for why he was thinking how desperately he *did* want to make Olivia pregnant. And how desperately he wanted to bind her to him forever. In whatever way he could. But when he joined her again on the bed, it was with the full knowledge that he would do no such thing. He would take whatever she was willing to offer him for now and give double that amount to her in return. And somehow, some way, he would make her realize how perfectly the two of them went together.

As he stretched out beside her, he hooked his thumb in the waistband of her panties and tugged them down over her legs, discarding them on the floor with his own clothing. Then he pulled her atop him again, cupping his hands over the heavy globes of her breasts, stroking her heated flesh until she moaned aloud with wanting him. When he felt her melting against him, he knew she was as ready for their union as he. Dropping his hands to her waist, he pushed her body backward and lifted her up over him, then raised himself and lowered her until their bodies began to join together.

It had been so long, Olivia thought as she luxuriated in the feel of Daniel's slow penetration. And she had never, ever, felt quite the way she did at that moment. With every solid inch of him that entered her, she lost a little more of herself to him, knowing that what she gave, she gave freely. He filled her—all of her. All the empty, lonely places that had lain dormant for so long, all the deep, fearful chasms that had languished untouched for what seemed like an eternity. Suddenly, Daniel was everywhere. And suddenly, Olivia never wanted to let him go.

Just as the realization permeated the sensual fog muddling her thoughts, he rolled so that she lay beneath him. Raising up on his elbows only far enough to keep from crushing the breath out of her, he retreated from inside her, then plunged in again, deeper this time than before. She clung to him, hooking her legs over his, clawing her way across his back to fold her arms over him in a fierce hug. Maybe, she thought, if she tried very, very hard, she could prevent him from ever leaving her.

And then she couldn't think at all. Because Daniel began to move against her again, building into a steady rhythm that carried them both over a roiling, tumultuous sea. Olivia, too, responded in kind, joining him jolt for jolt, thrust for thrust, parry for parry. Together, they reached for something beyond their knowledge or their dreams, and together, they found their way to the stars.

In a bolt of light that nearly blinded her, Olivia felt herself tumble over the edge, into a languishing kind of pleasure unlike anything she had ever known. She cried out at the same moment Daniel did, then felt him slump against her in completion. For long moments, they only lay entwined as a single being, their hearts pounding in perfect rhythm, their souls merged as one. She could do nothing but feel: the life of him still pulsing inside her, the sweat-soaked skin of his back beneath her fingers, the way he seemed to envelop her and shelter her from harm.

Daniel, her friend, had become her lover, she thought with a dreamy little smile as she tightened her arms around him. And all at once, her smile froze. Because only then did she allow herself to fully consider everything that had transpired that evening and what she had just done. Only then did she begin to comprehend what the results of her actions would be. And only then did she completely understand what a terrible crime she had committed.

"I have to leave," she blurted out suddenly, oblivious to how harsh her words would sound under the circumstances.

She felt Daniel go rigid in her arms before he braced his forearms on each side of her head and lifted himself up weakly to gaze down at her. His expression was edged with worry and more than a little anger. "I beg your pardon?" he asked.

Recognizing the fact that she had already pretty much decimated any chance for tenderness the two of them had now, Olivia figured her only alternative was to make her escape as quickly and efficiently as she possibly could. "I have to leave," she repeated, hoping her voice wasn't really as shaky as it sounded to her. "I have to go home."

"Why?"

He continued to tower over her and showed no indication that he meant to move, something that could create a problem for her in executing her escape plan. Still, this was Daniel, Olivia reminded herself. Not some big, burly biker, like Steve, who would more than likely ignore her request should she ask him to move.

"I...because...Zoey must be back with Simon by now," she said on a rush of words, "and I don't want to inconvenience her more than I already have."

He inhaled slowly and looked away, releasing his breath with some difficulty. When he turned to face her again, she could see that he was trying valiantly to fight off his anger.

"Livy, we just made love. I mean, we *just* made love. And I don't know about you, but it was pretty much as close to perfect as I've ever come. Yet all you can think about right now is inconveniencing your baby-sitter?"

She bit her lip nervously. "Well, that's not *all* I can think about."

He nodded. "I guess I can only hope that I'm one of the things you're thinking about, but there's no way in hell I'm going to ask you to tell me whether I am or not. I'm not sure I want to hear the answer."

"I'm thinking about you," she said softly, reluctantly threading her fingers through the damp hair at his temple. "And maybe...maybe that's the real reason I have to leave now."

His brows arrowed downward in confusion. "Why would thinking about me make you have to leave?"

She shook her head, wishing for the life of her that she could somehow explain. But how could she do that when she didn't yet understand her reaction herself? "It's kind of complicated, Daniel."

"Yeah, we make love and immediately you have to get home?" he asked angrily. "You're damned right it's complicated."

The fingers in his hair ceased their caresses, and she dropped her hand back to the bed. "Let me up, please."

Immediately, he rolled away from her, jackknifing up on the bed with his back to her. She reached out to touch him, thought better of the action and twisted her fingers together in her lap instead. When she dropped her gaze downward, she saw her clothing tangled with his in a heap on the floor, and her stomach knotted.

"This never should have happened," she said quietly.

He glanced back at her over his shoulder. "Why not?"

She reached for her underthings and struggled into them, trying not to feel self-conscious when he watched her intently as she dressed. Neither of them spoke as she awkwardly buttoned her dress. When she got to the top of the garment and realized she had missed a button somewhere along the way, she slumped forward, feeling defeated and tired and utterly confused.

"I asked you a question, Livy," Daniel said.

He was still seated at the edge of the bed, but that most intriguing part of him was hidden by a lump in the sheet. Olivia was both comforted and disappointed by the realization that he was so adequately covered. Yet still she did not reply to his query.

"Livy," he said again, his voice empty of the bitterness and anger that had punctuated it only a moment ago. Now he simply sounded tired and frustrated—almost, she thought, defeated. "What is it? What's wrong? Why are you leaving? Why do you say this never should have happened?"

"Because..." Her voice trailed off as she edged closer to the bedroom door, closer to escape. She paused there only a moment to look back at him. "It shouldn't have happened because... because..." She lifted a hand as if groping for something in midair that she was unable to find. Once more, she shook her head slowly and opened her mouth to explain, then fell silent. Finally she dropped her hand back to her side and her gaze to the floor, all the fight seeming to go out of her. "Because you mean too much to me," she said quietly, so quietly, he almost didn't hear her. "Don't you see that, Daniel? Don't you understand?"

And without waiting for a reply, she bolted from the door and down the stairs. She didn't hesitate for a second, even when he called her name out loudly behind her. And she didn't look back again.

Eight

It was over breakfast the following morning that Olivia was finally able to put her finger on what it was about making love with Daniel that had so thoroughly disrupted her peace of mind. She had lain awake for most of the night, staring into the darkness, feeling shaken and confused, wondering what on earth had possessed her to behave the way she had the night before. Simon seemed to have picked up on her unrest, too, because he had stayed awake fretting most of the night with her.

Now the baby dozed fitfully in his bassinet on the other side of the dining room, and Olivia sat in her nightgown staring into her tea. With her pounding head cradled in her hands, she wished for the life of her that the night before with Daniel had never happened. She was just beginning to talk herself into a better—if decidedly fake better—mood when the only thing that could make the morning even worse than it already was happened. There was a knock at her back door, followed by Daniel's breezy hello.

For a moment, she brightened, thinking that if he sounded so casual, then perhaps this morning was no different from any other. Maybe the past twelve hours had been nothing more than a dream, one of those amazingly erotic dreams like so many others she had experienced lately about her neighbor. Then she recalled how incredible she had felt for a little while the night before, how wonderfully animated Daniel had caused her to be for the first time in months. There was no way she could have dreamed those reactions, she thought. They had felt more real than anything else in her life.

"Livy?" he called out again. "Come on, I know you're home. Let me in. I need to talk to you."

Oh, and she could just guess what it was he needed to talk to her about, she thought. She looked down at her rumpled nightgown and robe and ran a shaky hand through her unkempt hair. Added to a sleepless night with a fussy baby, Olivia was certain she presented a less-than-attractive picture at the moment. For the first time since she had met him, she suddenly cared what Daniel thought about her looks, and she hated herself for it. It just went to prove she had been right about last night. The two of them never should have made love. It had ruined everything.

"I'm coming," she called out wearily, thinking it was too late for her to be worrying about her personal toilette now.

She shuffled to the back door and tugged it open to be greeted by Daniel and a crisp burst of morning sunshine. She squinted at the bright light, grumbling at the pain that shot through her head as a result. Without extending a verbal invitation, she moved aside to allow him in, then closed the door softly behind him.

"Are you okay?" he asked as he surveyed her. "You don't look so good this morning."

"Thanks a lot," she muttered, noting grudgingly that he looked as fresh and handsome as ever in his tight jeans and formfitting, faded purple polo shirt. "You always did know just the right thing to say to charm the socks off a girl."

He glanced down pointedly at the thick, gray gym socks she always slept in, summer or winter, and then back at her face with a crooked smile. "Doesn't look like I've quite succeeded yet," he said. "Good thing you weren't wearing socks last night."

She wanted to slap the jovial smugness off his face, but somehow refrained. "Don't you dare joke about that," she said softly, feeling her cheeks burn red.

He sobered immediately. "Joke about what?"

"You know perfectly well about what. That."

"What?"

She sighed impatiently. He wasn't going to let it rest, she thought. And of course, after what the two of them had shared together, she supposed that was to be expected. Still, she wasn't sure she was ready to talk about it just yet.

"Would you like a cup of tea or some coffee?" she asked evasively, moving away from him and toward the stove. "The water's still hot. It wouldn't take but a minute."

"No, thank you," he said, clearly disappointed by her cowardly retreat from the topic he had made clear he wanted to address. "I came over here to talk to you. I would have come last night, but I noticed Zoey's car was here until almost twelve. I didn't want to bother you that late."

Olivia removed her fingers from the handle of the tea-kettle and curled them into a fist at her side. Somehow she managed to keep herself from revealing that Daniel—at least thoughts of him—had bothered her well past midnight. "She was telling me about how all the nurses in the maternity ward are ready to mutiny because of some new intern at the hospital. The woman sounds like a real geek, which of course isn't unusual for interns, but . . . Makes me dread having to go back to work."

"So you and Zoey weren't talking about . . . us?"

Olivia shook her head, but looked away from his face. "I wasn't ready to talk about what happened. About . . . us."

He reached over and took her chin gently between his thumb and forefinger, then turned her head back so that she was forced to meet his gaze. "Are you ready to talk about us now?"

Reluctantly, she nodded, knowing that eventually the two of them would have to discuss what had happened. Putting it off would do nothing but create more tension between them. She motioned toward the living room after pointing at the sleeping baby in the bassinet. Daniel followed her, and she waited for him to sit. When he made himself comfortable on the sofa, she deliberately chose the chair opposite—and well away from—him. Tucking her feet up beneath her and wrapping her robe tightly around her, she waited for him to say something first.

"When I woke up this morning," he said, his gaze holding hers steady, "I thought I was waking up from the most wonderful dream I'd ever had. At first I was sure what had happened couldn't possibly have been anything *but* a dream, because it had been so perfect, something I'd been dreaming about for such a long time."

Olivia glanced away, unable to bear the sight of him looking at her so lovingly. Nevertheless, there was no way she could lie to him. "I thought it was a dream at first, too," she said softly.

"Then I remembered the way it ended," he continued as if she hadn't spoken, "and I knew I hadn't dreamed it at all. I realized what had happened between the two of us was all too real. Otherwise, I wouldn't have been feeling so...so damned betrayed. And I couldn't help but ask myself, 'Why?'" He paused for a moment, raking a big hand through his hair. When Olivia looked at him, he looked away. "Unfortunately," he continued quietly, "I'm not the one who can answer that question. Only you can do that." When he turned to face her again, his expression was hard, almost accusatory. "So I have to ask you, Livy. Why did you leave so abruptly last night? Why did you say what we shared together was a mistake?"

"Because it *was* a mistake," she told him, holding his gaze steady with her own. "It shouldn't have happened. I should have made sure it never happened."

"Why was that decision up to you? Don't I count for anything in this?"

At the note of pleading in his voice, she expelled a breath she had been unaware of holding. "Of course you count. But not in the way you think."

He looked dashed by her words. "Is that it? Do I mean so little to you?"

Without thinking, she rose from her chair and crossed the living room quickly, seating herself close beside him. She lifted a hand to touch his shoulder, hesitated for a moment, then carried through with the gesture, settling her fingers lightly against him. "No, Daniel, you've got it backward. You mean so *much* to me."

He looked at the hand pressing against his shoulder for a moment before covering it with his own. "If I mean so much to you, why did you bolt out of my house last night as if you couldn't get away from me fast enough?"

"I was scared," she told him honestly. "I was confused. I'm sorry, but I didn't know what else to do."

"I still don't understand."

She sighed fitfully, wondering how on earth she could explain her feelings to him without making things even worse. Finally she decided the direct route would probably be best. "You're my friend, Daniel. Don't you see? You're not like other men I've had in my life."

"Whoa, let me stop you there for a minute," he said as he lifted both hands before him to illustrate with a more literal gesture. "If this conversation is supposed to make me feel better, then it's only fair to warn you, Livy, that you're off to a really bad start."

She sighed again deeply, rested her forehead in her hand and tried again. "Every romantic relationship I've ever had with a man has ended badly," she said. "Every single one— all the way back to elementary school. When I get involved with someone romantically, something always goes wrong, and I always wind up getting hurt somehow."

She lifted her head again and stared him straight in the eye. "You . . . you're the first guy I've ever known who I've gotten along with this well. The only man I've ever been able to talk to without arguing, to spend time with without getting mad about something. You're the only man I know who doesn't end up making me feel bad about myself. And that can only be because you're my friend, and not my lover. If you and I keep up this way, all that will change. It will ruin everything we have together now. And I'm not willing to sacrifice something that good."

She squeezed his arm hard and placed her open palm over his cheek. "I don't want to lose you. Can't you understand that?"

Daniel watched her closely as she spoke, his heart sinking with every word she uttered. She honestly believed what she was telling him, he realized. She truly thought the reason she felt good when she was with him was simply because they were friends, and that love had absolutely nothing to do with it. He wondered if she even knew what love was. Wondered how she would react if he asked her about the possibility that she might just be in love with him as deeply as he was with her?

No, he couldn't do that, he decided. If he suggested something like that, she would just run screaming in terror in the opposite direction.

So what was he supposed to do? He wasn't about to let Olivia slip away from him this easily. She had just as much as told him that she loved him, hadn't she? Even if she didn't quite realize that yet.

But what if he was wrong? he wondered further. What if she really did only care for him as a close friend? What if she could never come to love him as she could other men, as he loved her? What would he do then? He couldn't very well go on living next door to her, witnessing her life from a distance while he fell more and more in love with her with every passing day. But the thought of not having her in his life at all was even worse. What was he supposed to do? he asked himself. Dammit, why couldn't she fall in love with him?

"You're not going to lose me," he said finally, hoping none of the turmoil boiling up inside him was audible in his voice. Still, he couldn't help himself when he said further, "But I don't understand why you think I'm not the kind of man you could share a healthy romantic relationship with."

She shook her head and smiled sadly. "You're just not my type, Daniel. I don't generally go for men like you."

What appeared to be her complete resignation in that statement troubled him. "And what kind of man am I?"

She didn't answer right away. For a moment she only looked at him longingly, as if she were honestly wishing things could be different between them. At last she told him, "You're stable. You're nice. Decent. Good."

"Oh, yeah, I can see why you wouldn't want a man like me in your life," he said sarcastically, his anger beginning to rise again.

She stood and paced the length of the room, obviously thinking hard about what she wanted to say next. "Look, I know it sounds crazy, but it's true. I like men who are...well, unstable. Unpredictable. Uncontrollable. Even out of control. The more dangerous they seem, the more I like them. Bad boys," she concluded with a helpless sigh. "I like bad boys. Guys who simply refuse to be bound by conventional or societal mores. They've had more experience with things. They've lived more colorful lives. They're more interesting."

When Daniel only stared at her, Olivia shrugged and paced back to the couch. "Men who ride motorcycles too fast without wearing their helmets," she clarified. "Men who go a couple of days without shaving and let their hair get too long. Who listen to their music too loud and drink their bourbon straight up. Men who drift from place to place and job to job. Men who challenge a woman," she concluded with a slight smile, her voice sounding much more animated now than it had when the two of them had begun their conversation.

Daniel stood, too, and frowned at her. "Men who knock you up and leave you alone to raise your kid. Is that it?"

Her smile fell. Unfortunately, she couldn't think of a single thing to contradict his assessment of the situation. So she only replied softly, "Touché."

"That's what you want in a man?" he asked, his voice growing louder despite his best efforts to keep it level. "Some 'bad boy' who has no regard for himself, or the rest of the world or the woman he's with?"

Olivia didn't much care for the way Daniel was interpreting her explanation, but for the life of her she couldn't come up with a better way to clarify what she meant. "Well . . ."

"Because that's exactly the kind of man you've just described, you know. A complete social moron who's more suited to the zoo than the company of human beings."

"That's not what I meant at all, and you know it," she shot back defensively. "What I just described is a man's man. The kind of guy a woman would want desperately to tame."

"To tame, huh?" he asked. "Like I said, a zoo denizen."

"A *jungle* denizen," she countered.

He nodded. "Right. Whatever. Well, now that I know what it is you want out of life, Livy—to be shoved aside and treated like next to nothing by some guy who'd rather watch monster trucks crunching school buses than talk about any future he might have with a woman—I guess you're right. I'm not the man for you. Because I *do* have a few plans for the future, and they all include a woman. But not a woman like you."

Her eyes widened in surprise at having the tables so quickly turned on her. "A woman like me?" she asked. "And just what kind of woman is that?"

"A woman who's too shortsighted and too immature to have any self-respect."

"What?" she asked incredulously. "Shortsighted? Immature?"

He nodded fiercely. "Because that's exactly what you are if you honestly feel the way you've just described."

Olivia opened her mouth to object to his charge, then decided his ridiculous notion wasn't worth responding to. She had plenty of self-respect. And she was *not* shortsighted, she assured herself. And she certainly wasn't immature. For Pete's sake, she was thirty-two years old, had been making it on her own for more than ten years and had been around the block more than a few times. If Daniel thought she was immature, then he was just a thickheaded fool.

"Then we're agreed," she said, crossing her arms defensively over her abdomen.

"About what?" he asked.

"That we're completely ill suited for each other," she told him. "That we both want totally different things out of life and are looking for mates who have nothing in common with what we perceive each other to be. That there's no way the two of us could ever survive any kind of romantic entanglement."

Daniel shook his head at her, still obviously wrapped up in his poorly conceived ideas about her, and folded his arms across his chest in much the same way she had. "As long as things stay like this," he said, "then, yeah, we're agreed that there's no way the two of us should get involved romantically."

"Fine," she said.

"Fine," he echoed.

"Good."

"Good."

"Just so we're in agreement."

"We're in agreement."

"Okay."

"Okay."

For a long moment they stood in the middle of the living room, legs braced apart, arms crossed, glaring at each other. The silence was almost deafening, Olivia thought, but she had no idea how to end it. Simon, however, seemed to have a very good idea what to do, because he chose that moment to cry out his irritation about something, and she hastily went to see to him.

"I think you better go," she told Daniel as she lifted the baby from his bassinet.

He nodded. "All right. My work here is done—that's for sure. There's not much reason for me to come around anymore, is there?"

She wished she could deny that, wished she could come up with any number of reasons why Daniel McGuane should come around every day for the rest of her life. But she'd just assured him there was no future in any romantic involvement between them, hadn't she? And after the heated discussion they'd just had—one in which the two of them had virtually insulted each other—she supposed there was even a chance now that their friendship might not ever recover completely. The realization bothered her more than she would have thought. Because as much as she had tried to set things to right, she had in fact only made them worse.

"No, I don't suppose there is," she replied reluctantly.

He opened his mouth to say more, but Simon opened his wider and began to wail. Evidently, Daniel had second thoughts about what he had been about to say and decided to keep quiet. He only looked at Olivia as she tried to soothe the irritable infant, and she found herself wishing more than anything that he would say whatever was on his mind.

But he turned away instead, and headed through the kitchen and out the back door without even saying goodbye. Simon began to cry louder then, and as much as she tried to comfort him, she found herself identifying completely with his distress. Sliding down into the corner of the dining room in a crumpled heap, Olivia rocked the sobbing

baby in her arms and succumbed to more than a few tears
of her own.

"So I told the guy, 'Look, if you don't like it, you don't
have to drink all of it, but I just invented Sylvie's Sensa-
tional Snarkhunt Surprise for Philadelphia's Most Creative
Bartender Contest next week, and I need an honest opinion.' Well, he took a really big sip, then asked me what was
in it. So I told him. Man, that first gulp he took came right
back up again, all over the bar, and believe me, Livy, a
Snarkhunt Surprise is *not* something you want to see a second time around." Sylvie paused for a thoughtful moment
before murmuring, "Must be the Surprise part. I was just
so sure the escargot garnish would be such a nice touch."

Olivia listened idly to the sound of her sister's voice, if not
precisely to what Sylvie was saying to her. To be polite,
however, she nodded her head in agreement to whatever it
was the other woman had proposed, and wondered what
Daniel McGuane was doing.

"Livy?" Sylvie asked, her words seeming to come from
a million miles away.

"Hmm?"

"Are you listening to me?"

"Mmm, hmm."

"I think she's been away from work too long," Olivia
heard Zoey comment. Her best friend, too, seemed to be
speaking as if from under water. "Her brain's turning into
cheese mold with nothing to challenge her but dirty diapers
and spit-up stains on her clothes."

"O-livia," Sylvie sang out softly, reaching across the
coffee table to tap her sister lightly on the temple. "Anybody home? Are you in there?"

"Sure, whatever," Olivia said, staring out the window of
her sister's Philadelphia high-rise apartment at the storm
clouds hovering over One Liberty Place.

"Push her harder," Zoey told Sylvie. Then she set her coffee mug down on the table and scooted closer to Olivia on the couch. "Here, I'll do it."

Olivia felt herself shoved to the left by a hand placed resolutely over her cheek. As she tumbled face first into the sofa cushion, she immediately snapped out of the reverie in which she'd been indulging. She rose back up, rubbed her cheek and glared at her best friend. "What did you do that for?"

"You were going stupid on us," Zoey said, lifting her coffee cup again. "You know how much we hate it when you do that."

The three women had met for Sunday brunch in the city and now indulged in after-brunch coffee and tea at Sylvie's. It was something the three of them tried to do at least once a month, but since the arrival of Simon, the particulars had been a little difficult for Olivia to orchestrate. She told herself it was nice finally being out and about again after months of being confined at home. But despite the animated conversation that had surrounded her all morning, she had contributed very little. Instead, she hadn't been able to do much but think about Daniel.

"Yeah," Sylvie agreed. "And you've been going stupid on us all day. Why is that?"

"I told you," Zoey said. "She's been away from work too long. When are you due back?"

"A couple more weeks," Olivia said with a sigh.

"You don't much sound like you're looking forward to it," Sylvie said.

"Actually, I am," Olivia told her, finally warming to the conversation somewhat. "I'm starting to go nuts being home alone with the baby every day. Not that Simon's any trouble, mind you," she added quickly, leaning over to kiss the baby settled comfortably in his Aunt Sylvie's lap. "But those daytime talk shows are really starting to bring me down."

Sylvie nodded. "Yeah, I know what you mean. Working nights like I do, I see more than my share of those things. Did you catch the one last week about the transsexual hockey groupies who married cross-dressing serial killers without knowing it?"

Olivia nodded. "What's really scary is that I actually sat through the entire show."

"Yeah, me too."

"Boy, that is scary," Zoey said, shaking her head at both of them. "We should have gotten together long before today. You guys clearly aren't getting out enough."

Neither Olivia nor Sylvie disputed the comment.

"So what's the story with Daniel McGuane?" Zoey asked in a not-so-subtle effort to change the subject.

Olivia started violently at the question, as if she'd been poked by a cattle prod. The reaction caused her to slosh a good bit of her tea over the cup and onto her hand, and she busied herself fussing with a napkin to clean up the mess instead of answering.

"He's as yummy as ever," Sylvie responded for her sister when Olivia so clearly tried to duck the question. She leaned toward Zoey and whispered loudly, "If you ask me, I think Livy has a crush on him."

"I do *not* have a crush on him," Olivia was quick to object.

Sylvie ignored her and continued to address Zoey in a loud stage whisper. "You should have seen the shameless way she was drooling over him the last time I was at her house when he was there. She was positively frothing at the mouth."

"I was not," Olivia denied indignantly.

Zoey, too, seemed to have forgotten Olivia was there, because she whispered loudly back to Sylvie, "I baby-sat for her a couple of weeks ago while she had dinner with him, and when she came home, she looked awfully... you know... mussed."

"Mussed?" Olivia repeated. "I wasn't mussed. Was I?"

"And she never did tell me what happened while she was over there," Zoey added pointedly. "When I asked her if she'd had a good time with him, do you know what she said?"

Sylvie adopted a positively scandalous expression. "No, what?"

Zoey looked suspiciously from side to side, as if fearful of being overheard. "She said . . . she said, 'It was fine.'"

"No!" Sylvie cried.

Zoey nodded. "Yes. I was shocked, too."

"All right, you guys." Olivia interrupted the byplay. "Knock it off."

The two women dropped the gossipy matron routine and leaned back in their seats to eye her speculatively.

"Well, then?" Zoey finally asked. "What happened? For a while there, you were talking about Daniel all the time. But lately, you haven't uttered one word about the guy."

"For a while there he was coming to my house every day to fix the back porch," Olivia pointed out. "Now the work is finished, so he's not coming around anymore. It's that simple."

Sylvie placed an index finger against her cheek thoughtfully. "Hmm. Now why don't I believe it's quite as simple as you say?"

"I *know* I don't believe it's that simple," Zoey stated. "You looked more than mussed when you came barreling into the house that night after you had dinner with Daniel, Livy. You looked scared to death. Just what the hell happened between the two of you that night?"

It was going to come out eventually, Olivia thought. She'd never kept a secret from Sylvie and Zoey, just as they had never kept a secret from her. It was what made their three-way friendship so solid. Even if she didn't tell them about making love with Daniel, they'd find out somehow. The three women were almost telepathic in that sense.

"We made love that night," Olivia said softly, unable to look at either of her companions.

"I knew it," Zoey said triumphantly. "That's wonderful. You've finally fallen for a nice, decent guy who'll do right by you. This calls for a celebration."

"Whoa, whoa, whoa," Olivia said, holding up her hands in protest. "No celebration."

"Why not?" Sylvie asked. "Zoey's right. This is truly a banner day when you forsake those goons you normally see for a guy like Daniel."

"What happened with Daniel and me that night won't be happening again," Olivia said simply. "Making love, I mean. Daniel and I are both in agreement about that."

"What?!" the two women chorused.

"Why not?" Sylvie asked.

"Because it was a mistake," Olivia told them. "Daniel's not my type, and I'm not his. That's all there is to it. We both realize that now, and we won't be seeing each other... that way... again."

"But—" Zoey objected.

"I don't want to talk about it," Olivia said.

"Oh, Livy, I should have known you'd do something to mess it up," Sylvie muttered as she slumped back in her seat in a clear display of disappointment.

"Me?" she exclaimed. "What Daniel and I had was a mutual parting of the ways. Why am *I* always the one to blame when things go wrong in my life?"

"Because it's always your fault," Sylvie told her. "You're a very self-destructive person in your own way, Livy. If something went wrong with you and Daniel before the two of you even gave it a chance, then it's because *you* did something to foul it up."

"Oh, some supportive sister you are."

"She's right, Liv," Zoey interjected. "You do tend to get yourself into some bad situations sometimes."

"Me?" Olivia repeated. Then with a deep sigh, she relented somewhat. "Okay, I admit that I wind up in some pretty major messes sometimes."

"Sometimes?" Sylvie echoed incredulously. "Livy, you're *always* in some kind of mess. And it almost always involves some creepy guy."

Olivia waved a hand at her sister negligently. "So maybe I haven't met Mr. Right yet. But I'm not responsible if things keep falling apart in my life. I do the best I can, and things always go wrong anyway. That's not my fault."

"Then whose fault is it?" Sylvie asked.

"Circumstances' fault, that's who," Olivia replied quickly.

"If it's just circumstances, then why does it happen so often?" Zoey wanted to know.

"Because I'm unlucky, that's why," Olivia assured her.

Both women shook their heads at her in obvious disappointment.

"Oh, Livy," Sylvie said sadly, "you just don't get it at all, do you?"

"Get what?" Olivia asked.

But her sister only continued to shake her head in silent reproach.

"Give her time, Sylvie," Zoey said as she lifted her coffee for another sip. "She'll figure it out. Eventually."

"Figure what out?" Olivia demanded.

But Zoey, too, seemed unwilling to elaborate. Instead, she and Sylvie exchanged knowing looks before turning their attention back to their coffee.

"I know she'll figure it out," Sylvie said finally. "I just hope it's not too late when she does."

Nine

Time seemed to pass extremely slowly after that, July creeping into August as if tied to a huge, reluctant rock. An unbearable heat had shimmered over south Jersey for most of the month, but by mid-August it seemed to rain every day for a week. A cold front swept down from the north and settled over the Delaware Valley for what seemed like an eternity, bringing with it wet, windy, cool days completely inappropriate for summer. But Olivia didn't mind the change at all. Because the weather outside reflected perfectly her emotions inside—drab, dreary, depressing.

Since Daniel had finished her back porch, the little addition had become her sanctuary. She had refurnished it with some secondhand yard sale wicker and dozens of plants in every variety and size. She had looked forward to spending the better part of her last days home from work out on her porch among them, reading, relaxing and simply enjoying time with her son. But thanks to the uncooperative weather, she found herself trapped indoors instead. Trapped indoors where she could do nothing but stare out the living room window at the house next door to hers, waiting for even the slightest glimpse of her neighbor, and missing his presence in her life more than she ever would have guessed she could.

But Daniel seldom seemed to be at home these days. She assumed he had gone back to work, perhaps even at a location somewhere out of town. She had no way of knowing for certain since he had seemed intent on avoiding her completely after their last disastrous encounter. He may have even met someone, she pondered—some nice, decent, stable woman who would be perfectly suited to him and who could fully appreciate what he had to offer. Perhaps he had taken to spending the majority of his time with her.

The thought should have comforted Olivia, should have made her rejoice that so deserving a man as Daniel had found a woman to love who loved him back. But the thought did not set well with her. Not at all. So she shrugged it off and tried not to think more about it, and instead made every effort to keep herself occupied watching the changes in her son as he grew.

Simon was amazing. And he was her salvation during the days that followed Daniel's departure from her life. By the time he reached thirteen weeks of age, he seemed to have doubled his birth weight. He was growing so quickly that there were times when she was sure she could hear his bones stretching. No longer did he simply lie in his bouncer or crib simply staring at her as if she were responsible for nothing more in life than providing him with amusement. Now he was developing a personality, and he smiled and cooed and often squealed with laughter. He made a lot of noise, just because he knew he could, and he seemed to be a perpetual motion machine. He was a very happy baby. And Olivia was a very happy mom.

But not a particularly happy woman. Even on the days when Simon brought her nothing but joy and laughter, there was still one slight problem that continued to preoccupy her.

Well, not exactly slight, she amended late one Thursday afternoon as she stared out at the gray rain pattering against the grass between her house and her next door neighbor's. One couldn't exactly call six-foot-two and two hundred pounds of solid masculine flesh *slight*. Not when it came wrapped in a package like Daniel McGuane.

As the thought formed, the lights in her living room flickered and died, and Olivia was left standing in the pale, dun-colored illumination of the late afternoon. Not again, she thought miserably, recalling the last time her power had gone out. That had been nearly three months ago, the night Daniel had come over to check on her and Simon, the night her porch had collapsed beneath the weight of a mighty oak. The night that had been the beginning of everything that had since gone awry.

She closed her eyes for a moment and remembered those utterly peaceful moments when she had been nursing Simon in her nearly silent living room as Daniel looked on and chatted with her. She had teased him about his concern for the baby, and had thanked him for worrying about them both. He had behaved almost like a father that night, she thought. Almost like a husband. And somehow, for those few moments, everything in the world had seemed to be right.

She was about to turn away from the window when she saw Daniel's aged, but sensible, four-door station wagon pull into the driveway next door. She supposed it was a practical vehicle for him to drive, something that allowed him to transport the tools necessary for his work with a minimum of fuss. Nevertheless, he was the only single man she knew who drove a car like that. Most unmarried men would shun the very thought of even owning a station wagon, let alone driving one, horrified that someone might think them...ugh...*family men*. But not Daniel. She wouldn't even be surprised to one day see him driving up in that epitome of suburban chariots—the minivan. Such a vehicle didn't seem at all incongruent for him. She wondered why.

She watched as he pushed open the driver's-side door and leapt out, then angled her head to the side for a better view as he sprinted toward his front door with an oversize toolbox bouncing effortlessly in his grasp. She knew the lacy curtains covering her window would hide her flagrant espionage now that the lamps had gone out with the electricity, but she still took an involuntary step backward when Daniel suddenly looked up from his porch to gaze directly at her house. For a long moment he only stood there watching, staring right into the window where she stood as if he were looking directly into her eyes.

He knew she was there, she thought. He knew she was watching him. She didn't know how she knew it—or how he knew it for that matter—but he knew.

He stood completely still for long moments with his keys in his hand, as if he were weighing some serious consideration. For those moments, she held her breath and remained motionless, and it seemed as if time stopped moving forward. Then Daniel looked away, unlocked his front door and went inside. Olivia released her breath with a long sigh, and moved quickly away from the window.

This had gone on long enough, she thought, this distance the two of them had created between themselves. They were friends, dammit, good friends. So they had forgotten about that for one night and things had gotten a little out of hand. So they had made love. So what? These were the nineties, for Pete's sake, the end of the twentieth century. Sex was no big deal. It was everywhere a person went—in books and movies, on TV. They even used sex to sell power tools. It was nothing these days. Nothing at all.

Just because two people went to bed together, it didn't mean everything had to change, did it? Olivia thought. There was no reason why she and Daniel couldn't go back to being friends, go back to the way things had been before. They just had to put this chapter in their relationship behind them and forget it had ever happened. They just needed to talk about it and let it go, that was all.

She glanced over at the baby who lay beneath his busy gym on a quilt in the middle of the living room floor, swatting at elephants and giraffes. "Everything's going to be all right, Simon," she assured him quietly. "What do you think about making a little visit next door to see Daniel, hmm?"

The baby smiled and laughed and kicked his legs vigorously, flailing his arms in the air. Immediately, Olivia responded by picking him up, then lifted him high above her before bringing him down to nuzzle his neck and cheek. Simon laughed harder.

"So what do you say, buddy?" she asked him as she curled her arms beneath him and held him so that his face was level with hers. "You want to go for a little walk?"

Simply by noting his expression, Olivia knew what his answer would be. He was almost as eager to see Daniel again as she was. Almost. So, bundling the baby up in a hooded sweatshirt and tiny high-top sneakers, she set off for the house next door.

Daniel tossed his toolbox with a loud clatter onto the scarred Formica top of his kitchen table, and sighed with much enthusiasm. His day had been a truly lousy one, but then, that wasn't at all unusual lately. He couldn't remember the last time he'd had a *good* day. Oh, wait a minute, yes, he could. His last good day had been the one that had ended with him making love to Olivia Venner. Come to think of it, though, he amended as he thought further about that day, that one had ended pretty badly, too.

For the past three weeks he had thrown himself body and soul into a new job, rising before the sun and working well into the night just to keep himself away from home as much as possible. A couple of dinks—"double-income, no kids" types—had bought a rickety old Victorian in nearby Haddonfield and were refurbishing it from top to bottom. An old friend of his had been hired to oversee most of the labor, and had called Daniel to see if he'd be interested in doing some interior work for a change. And considering the way the weather had been behaving lately, he'd been grateful for the change. He'd been grateful, too, that the house had been such a wreck and the labor so demanding. It had provided him with a much needed diversion to keep his mind off Olivia for a while.

But only for a little while. Because the moment he packed up his hammer and level at the end of the day, Daniel's thoughts immediately wandered into territory he'd rather leave unexplored. Inevitably, he would recall things, like the way Olivia had looked sleeping so soundly in his bed that morning after the storm, or her indignant expression when she'd defended the manufacturers of white bread. Sometimes, out of nowhere, he would remember her genuinely happy smile to discover that he had been the one to share Simon's triumph with the maple leaf, and the image of her surrounded by a pool of golden light as she fed her son.

And Simon. Boy, did Daniel miss that kid. Who would have thought that a baby—a *baby* for God's sake—would usurp such a big place in his heart? Until he'd met Simon, Daniel had never much thought about kids before, had really never even been around them. Then, within a matter of weeks, days even, his life had suddenly been filled by the presence of one.

He didn't pretend to understand why he had fallen for that baby so hard, so fast. Simon was in no way related to him, despite Olivia's plea that Daniel be there for her son when the little guy needed some masculine guidance. Yet the baby had roused in him some of the fiercest emotions he had ever experienced. Fondness for the kid, certainly, but there was more to it than that. He felt protective of Simon, and anxious to steer him in the right direction. Hell, what could he say? He loved the little guy.

And as much as he cared for Simon, he was even more bedeviled by the feelings he still carried around for the little guy's mom. Despite everything that had happened—the abrupt, unsettling end to the lovemaking he and Olivia had shared, and the angry words the two of them had exchanged shortly afterward—Daniel still loved her deeply. And dammit, he knew she cared for him, too. That was what made the whole episode so frustrating. He wished there were some way he could make Olivia open her eyes to the way things could be between them. If only he could show her how unfairly she was behaving, how much she was cheating them both.

God, a beer would be good right about now, he thought as he lifted a hand to ease a knot at the back of his neck. Or better yet, a straight shot of bourbon. There was no reason why he couldn't turn around and go right back outside, get in his car and speed to the nearest dive, then spend the night drinking cheap booze, listening to Bruce Springsteen sing about cars and feeling up whatever faceless woman happened to conveniently seat herself at the stool beside his at the bar.

That was how he used to ease the tension of a crummy day, he reminded himself. Hell, if it had worked before, it would no doubt work again. Who cared what he did with his life? Two years of clean living had brought him what? Diddly-squat, that's what. For the past few weeks, he'd been on a steady decline anyway. He'd forsaken his weights completely, because he simply couldn't dispel the image of Olivia in a sweat-soaked tank top and shorts lying prone on the opposite side of the room. His diet had been lousy, composed of carry-out food and whatever he could find to be delivered in the middle of the night, because he just hadn't much cared about what he consumed, as long as it put an end to his hunger. A quick jaunt down to the local pub for a brew and a bleary all-nighter seemed a logical next step.

Only a quick rap at his back door prevented Daniel from carrying out his plan. He sighed at being so thwarted, looked down with a frown at his filthy denim overalls and faded red T-shirt, then shrugged philosophically. Whoever had come calling was visiting without an invitation, he thought, so they could damn well suffer his workday dishevelment. Hell, what had he just said? He didn't care anymore.

Until he opened his back door to find Olivia Venner standing on his threshold, holding her son in her arms.

Then immediately, Daniel swept a hand through his sweat-streaked hair and brushed at bits of sawdust that spattered him front and back. Olivia looked clean and crisp in her tight jeans and lavender sweatshirt, her cheeks pink from the cool air outside, her dark eyes more dazzling than he recalled. For long moments they only stared at each other in silence. Then Simon seemed to grow bored with the game and squealed.

The sound seemed to snap Olivia out of her trance, because she shifted the baby to her other side so that Simon could get a better view of Daniel. "Hi," she said quietly.

"Hi," he replied just as softly.

"I...I saw you drive up, and...and since it's been awhile since I saw you, I thought I'd come over and see what you were up to. I—" She broke off and looked down at the baby, whose gaze was fixed fast to Daniel. "We," she started again, "we just wanted to say hello."

"Come on in," he said, stepping aside to allow them entry.

As they passed him, Simon still stared at him intently, his expression studious, as if he knew Daniel from somewhere but couldn't quite place his face. The red sweatshirt's hood was tied snugly about his face, giving him the appearance of a chubby elf. Then he suddenly broke into a wide, toothless smile, and Daniel laughed.

"Can I hold him?" Daniel asked Olivia after he'd closed the door behind them.

"Sure," she said, relinquishing her burden to him without hesitation.

He was much heavier than he'd been the last time Daniel had held him. "Jeez, I can't get over how big he's gotten," he said, hefting the little guy against his shoulder. He loosened the bow beneath the baby's chin and pushed back his hood. "And still as bald as a cue ball," he remarked further, running his palm over the soft, downy fuzz that was nearly invisible on Simon's head. "That's amazing."

"He'll get hair eventually," Olivia assured him. "At least I think he will. Eventually. Someday."

Daniel laughed and started to hand the baby back. "I'm a mess. I shouldn't be holding him."

But Olivia declined to take her baby from him, noting as well as Daniel did how comfortable Simon seemed to be in his grasp. "You've got to be kidding," she said. "You think *you're* a mess? You've got nothing on the mess a baby can create, trust me." She smiled and leaned over to kiss Simon on the cheek. "Besides, he's having a good time. He's missed having you around."

Daniel wanted to ask her if Simon was the only one who'd missed having him around, but he refrained. Instead he pulled a chair away from the kitchen table and invited Olivia to make herself comfortable, then took his own seat beside her, sitting Simon up on the table between them with his hands over the baby's belly and back, keeping him propped in place.

"He's changed a lot since the last time I saw him," he said. "I guess from here on out, it's just one growing spurt after another."

Olivia nodded. "I know. Sometimes when I go to get him out of the crib in the morning, I'd swear he's grown an inch overnight. It's spooky."

Simon, oblivious to the fact that he was the topic of conversation, leaned forward against Daniel's hand, reached around the barrier of strong fingers holding him up to grab at his shoelace, then tried to eat his shoe.

"He's developing a lot of oral fixations lately, too," Olivia said with a laugh.

When she reached over and tried to sit the baby back up again, her hand fell over Daniel's. Instantly, he was reminded of how soft and warm she was, of how her fingers had felt skimming lightly—and at times, not so lightly—over his bare flesh. More than anything, he wanted to cover her hand with his and draw it to his mouth. Simon wasn't the only one with oral fixations, he thought. And Olivia's hands weren't the only things he had on his mind for fixing upon.

She seemed to read his thoughts, because she quickly snatched her hand away. When she spoke again, her voice was low and a little shaky, as if she, too, were recalling the single sensuous encounter they had shared. "The drool mechanism has begun to function effectively, too," she said, wiping Simon's face with a hanky she withdrew from her sleeve, "and now everything he picks up goes straight to the mouth."

Daniel laughed. "Hey, he's a baby. That's his job. In fact, if you look at his job description, you'll find drooling listed as a requirement right after blowing a raspberry when Mommy's trying to impress her friends with his accomplishments."

Olivia chuckled. "Yeah, he does that, too. How did you know?"

Daniel flushed. "I, ah, I've been doing some reading about babies."

She smiled, clearly both surprised and delighted by his revelation. "You have?"

"Yeah."

"Why?"

He shrugged. "I don't know. I was just interested."

"You know, I bet there are a lot of fathers out there who don't even do that."

He flushed harder. "Livy, I don't want you to think I'm going to try and use Simon to insinuate myself into your life. I'll still be more than happy to be here for him when he needs me. But I know how you feel about me. I know you don't want me to—"

"No," she cut him off. "That's not what I think at all. What I said I meant as a compliment. And I do want you in my life, Daniel. So does Simon, obviously."

The baby was leaning forward again, staring straight ahead, but opening his mouth as he approached his shoe. Daniel tried to focus his attention on keeping the little guy's feet well away from his face, and told himself not to place too much stock in what Olivia was telling him. Friends, he reminded himself. That's all she wanted to be.

Although he continued to attend to the baby, he couldn't help himself when he asked her, "Livy, why did you come over?"

When she didn't reply, he looked up at her, only to find her gazing back at him with an expression of complete confusion. "Because..." she began, her voice laced with uncertainty. "Because...because..." She sighed deeply, slumped back in her chair and seemed to surrender to herself. "Because I miss you, Daniel. That's why."

"Do you?"

"Yes."

He thought for a moment before replying, wondering just how much of himself he should reveal to her. And although his next words were offered for Olivia, he continued to watch the baby when he spoke. Finally he said quietly, "You know, it's funny you should say that, because I miss you, too."

"Really?"

He nodded slowly, yet still didn't look at her. "But something tells me I've been missing you in a much different way than you have me."

"What...what do you mean?"

She sounded confused and a little wary. When he looked up, she was watching him curiously, and all he wanted to do was haul her out of her chair and into a fierce embrace. He wanted to carry her up the stairs as he had that night so many weeks ago, then make love to her over and over until the only place it felt right to be was in each other's arms. He wanted to tell her that he loved her. And he wanted to hear her tell him she loved him, too.

Instead, he covered the baby's ears with his hands and fought to keep his voice steady as he told her, "What I've missed most, Livy, is touching you. And not in the way you'd think. Although God knows I still lay awake at night remembering how you felt naked beneath me, the way your fingers felt closing over me to draw me inside you, the way your skin seemed to catch fire when I opened my hand over your—"

"Daniel, please..." Olivia whispered with a groan, her face flushing hotly, her eyes blazing with some unknown fire.

He inhaled a shaky breath and removed his hands from Simon's ears, who now sat and looked at him in confusion. But he only continued to eye Olivia and went on relentlessly, "What I miss even more than that are all are the simple, harmless little ways you touched me every day when I was at your house. The way you used to open your hand over my back to let me know you were coming up behind me. Or how you always squeezed my forearm when you were excited about something Simon had done and wanted me to come and see. Even the few times you curled your fingers over my shoulder to keep your balance when you tiptoed through the back porch before I'd finished laying the floor. That's what I miss most of all, Livy. Just being with you on a daily basis."

She was still blushing, but her color had faded to a delicate pink. Nevertheless, her eyes seemed to burn and her lips were parted, as if she were recalling as well as he every image he had described. "That's what I miss, too," she said softly. "Just having you around."

He nodded. "But do you also miss the other things? The evening we spent together, the strength of our lovemaking, the way we made each other feel, even if just for a little while?"

She looked panicked by the question, her eyes straying from his to the baby. Gingerly she reached for Simon, pulling him into her lap as if her son might protect her from any future plundering Daniel might have on his mind. The baby looked over his shoulder at Daniel with an inquisitive expression, then turned back to lean into his mother. Olivia fussed with straightening his clothes, her voice sounding quiet despite the troubling nature of her words.

"I, um, I haven't really given that night much thought," she said.

"Oh, no?"

She shook her head and continued to look at the baby. "No."

"It meant nothing to you?"

She chuckled, a nervous little sound, but still didn't look at him. "It was all right, I guess."

"But not as exciting as other times," he surmised skeptically with an arched brow. "Not as exciting as it was with other men."

She lifted her shoulders in an awkward shrug. "Not really."

"So you've had lots of other lovers, then, to compare me with."

She began to flush all over again. "Well, no, not exactly...."

"But enough that you were immediately assured that I was in no way the type of lover you like."

"I suppose..."

"I wasn't *bad* enough for you. Is that it?"

She bit her lip, finally lifted her head to meet his gaze, then quickly looked away again. "Um, no. No, I guess you weren't."

He sat studying her in silence for a long time, knowing she was lying through her teeth, but having no idea how to make her admit that to either him or herself. Finally he stood, then went to the back door and opened it.

"I think it might be better if you left now," he said.

When she snapped her head up to look at him, he could see that she was shocked and felt utterly betrayed. His stomach knotted into a great fist. God, she looked as if he'd slapped her or something.

"Well, you did just insult my sexual technique," he pointed out. "Most men need at least a few minutes alone to get over something like that."

"I didn't mean—"

"Now, Livy," he stated. "I think you should leave now."

She set Simon on the kitchen table and lifted his hood over his head, but left the strings dangling loose, clearly unwilling to take any longer than she had to. Hefting the baby against her left shoulder, she looked at Daniel one final time, appeared to want to tell him something, then looked away without saying a word.

As she rushed by him, he reached out and circled her wrist with strong fingers, halting her flight before she could escape. When she turned, he bent his head toward her, covering her mouth with his in what he had intended to be a brutal, hurtful kiss. But it was impossible for him to kiss Olivia in such a way. Instead he moved his lips gently against hers, feeling her soften and grow warm beneath him in exactly the same way he responded to her. He dropped a hand to her waist and pulled her closer, touching his tongue lightly to a corner of her mouth.

Just as he was about to take fuller advantage of the embrace, he felt a tiny hand on his cheek, and his eyes fluttered open. Simon, who had been leaning over Olivia's shoulder, had turned and was watching Daniel kiss his mother. He had one hand on Daniel's face and one on Olivia's. And he was smiling. Smiling as if he couldn't be more pleased with what was clearly, to him at least, a wonderful development.

Daniel pulled away and took the baby's hand in his, but his gaze was trained steadfastly on Olivia. "Can you get a sitter for Simon Saturday night?" he asked her.

She still looked a little dazed from his kiss—a very good sign, Daniel thought—but she nodded slowly. "I think Sylvie's off this weekend. If she's not, Zoey said she's always available."

"Then call one or the other," he told her. "Because I've got something to show you Saturday night, Livy. Something you've never seen before. Something, with any luck at all, you'll never see again." He sighed, running a big hand through his hair with much agitation. "Something you're not likely to forget anytime soon," he concluded, his voice sounding weary.

"What's that?"

"Just make the call. I'll pick you up at seven."

Ten

In fact, both Sylvie and Zoey showed up to baby-sit for Simon on Saturday night. Sylvie had stopped by Big Bob's Videorama on the way to the house, and had rented a double feature of *Beach Blanket Biceps* and *Beefcake County Jail* for when Simon had turned in for the night. Zoey, evidently having a similar idea, brought with her copies of *Howard's End* and *Cries and Whispers*. Olivia shook her head hopelessly at the two, knew that somewhere along the line they would reach a compromise, and fixed them both dinner.

"So you have another date with Daniel," Zoey said as she bounced Simon in her lap. She threw a waist-length, fire-orange braid over her shoulder to keep it from the baby's grasp. "And after assuring us that there was absolutely nothing of a romantic nature between the two of you. Well, my, my, my, my, my. This *is* beginning to get interesting."

"It's not a date," Olivia said adamantly. "He just said he has something to show me."

Sylvie grinned lasciviously. "I can only imagine what that might be. You've seen all of him already, haven't you?"

"Only in the dark," Olivia replied before she could stop herself. She clapped a hand over her mouth to prevent herself from saying any more.

The other women chuckled heartily.

"If I had Daniel McGuane all to myself," Zoey said, "you can bet I'd turn on every light in the house so I could see every solid inch of him. Remember that time we were all out in the backyard and he came home from work wearing nothing but those raggedy overalls with no shirt and his big ol' steel-toed work boots? And he had that leather tool belt hanging low around his hips with all his little tools attached. Remember that?"

Sylvie shivered with delight. "Who could forget? I still have fantasies about what it would have been like to walk over and unhook every metal fixture on his clothing."

Zoey nodded, her expression dreamy. "Yeah. With my teeth."

Sylvie gaped. "You, too?"

The other woman nodded. "It would be worth every cap."

"All right, you guys," Olivia said, "knock it off. You're getting more drool on the floor than Simon does."

Zoey and Sylvie snapped out of their reverie and turned their attention to Olivia.

"You're not actually going to wear *that* tonight, are you?" Sylvie asked, indicating her sister's faded blue jeans and blousy white peasant top.

Olivia glanced down at her clothes and nodded. "Sure. What's wrong with this?"

"Where's he taking you?" Zoey asked.

"I don't know. He didn't say."

"Then you *definitely* don't want to wear that," Sylvie said.

"Why not?"

Sylvie sighed melodramatically, clearly appalled by her older sister's lack of social graces. "Because, Livy, when a guy doesn't tell you where he's taking you, it means he's taking you someplace really special. So you should wear something nice." She paused thoughtfully for a moment before adding, "Of course, in your case, that means you should wear one of the things that I loaned you."

"But—"

"The yellow dress," Sylvie decided immediately.

Olivia paled. "Oh, I don't think so. That dress is so... so... I mean, there's hardly any back to it at all, and the front is cut way down to... It's just too revealing," she finally concluded.

"You mean sexy," her sister corrected her.

"Inappropriate," Olivia tried again.

"Perfect," Sylvie assured her. "Now march upstairs and change right now. And do something else with your hair. And, jeez, how about just a little lipstick for a change, huh?" When Olivia hesitated, she swept her hands in a shooing gesture toward the stairs. "Hurry up. Daniel will be here in fifteen minutes."

Reluctantly, Olivia did as her sister requested. As she left the kitchen, she heard Sylvie tell Zoey, "Frankly, I don't know how we both resulted from the same gene pool. The woman is absolutely hopeless where men and fashion are concerned. I mean really..."

Olivia came back downstairs just as the doorbell grated out a tinny squeal. She had followed her sister's instructions to the letter and now wore the little yellow sundress that looked—in her opinion anyway—far more provocative when Sylvie wore it than it did now. She had swept her unruly dark curls back with two mother-of-pearl combs and hooked a pearl choker around her neck. She had even donned a little lipstick in a delicate shade of coral, just so she wouldn't have to listen to Sylvie's complaining anymore.

But when she rounded the hallway corner to enter the living room and found Daniel standing just inside the front door waiting for her, she wondered if maybe her sister wasn't quite as savvy in the dating department as she pretended to be. Because if Daniel's neglect in telling her where the two of them would be going tonight meant he was taking her someplace special, then that someplace special was extremely casual.

In fact, she thought as she surveyed him further, not only was he dressed down for the occasion, but he was dressed lower than she'd ever seen him dressed before, surpassing even his tattered work clothes. Instead of his usual faded, but clean blue jeans, he wore a ragged, oil-stained pair of dungarees that were more tear than denim. His black T-shirt was more of the same, only the stains weren't quite as obvious thanks to the dark color. Over that he wore a black leather biker jacket that boasted a number of scrapes and tears, as if it had barely protected him from more than one nasty spill on a bike. But it was Daniel's face that distressed Olivia most of all. Because although she could easily dismiss his attire as some silly joke, his expression was anything but funny.

She could tell he hadn't shaved since the last time she'd seen him. Instead of the smooth, sleek hollows beneath his sharp cheekbones that she had always been tempted to trace with her fingertips, his skin was covered by the scruffy, dark stubble of a two-day-old beard. His sandy hair, normally tamed with a comb except for the one stray piece that always wanted to fall over his forehead, was swept back now by some gooey hair oil that made it seem darker in color. But his eyes were what Olivia noticed most of all. Daniel's eyes—eyes that normally looked upon her with affection and laughter—were bleak and stormy and full of animosity.

All in all, she decided, he looked like some rough, rowdy, undisciplined street punk. He looked ... bad. And Olivia didn't like it. She didn't like it at all.

"Daniel?" she said by way of a greeting. She tried to make light of the situation, but her voice was strained when she asked, "Is that you under there?"

"Let's go," was all he said in reply. He yanked open the door behind him and preceded her through it, out into the evening twilight without further comment.

She supposed she was meant to follow him, but he hadn't so much as acknowledged her presence in any way. He hadn't even said hello to Simon, she realized, and that just wasn't like Daniel at all. Olivia exchanged wary, confused looks with Zoey and Sylvie, who seemed as mystified as she by what had just transpired. But all they offered her in explanation were two blank expressions and puzzled shakes of their heads.

"Uh, have a good time?" Sylvie said in farewell.

Zoey nodded, then reached into her pocket and extracted a quarter. "Here," she said, thrusting it into Olivia's hand. "You might need this. My aunts always made sure I never left the house with a boy without giving me the extra coin for a phone call. And don't put it in your purse," she added when Olivia moved to do just that. "Put it somewhere on your person, just in case. They made me do that, too. And it's a good thing they did."

Normally, Olivia would have told her friend she was being silly. But this time, she silently nodded her thanks and tucked the quarter into the pocket of her dress.

"And don't stay out too late," Zoey called after her as Olivia followed Daniel's path out the door.

What she discovered outside about him was every bit as surprising and confounding as what she had seen of him inside. Instead of in his car, he sat straddling a huge Harley-Davidson hog. She had never seen him on a motorcycle before and knew for a fact that he didn't own one. Nevertheless, he looked perfectly natural perched atop the big machine, as if he had been born to be wild with the best—or maybe the worst—of them.

As she cautiously approached, she noticed something else that was strange. Daniel was smoking, something that was completely at odds with his stay-healthy life-style. And not just smoking, she noted, but sucking quite heartily on the end of a cigarette, holding the smoke deep inside his lungs for several moments before exhaling with a slow, smooth release of white. This wasn't an affectation, she thought. He was serious about his unfiltered cigarette.

"You coming or not?" he asked her, flicking the remainder of the cigarette onto the driveway and stubbing it out with the toe of his black leather boot. "We don't have all night, you know. Let's go."

"Can't we take your car instead?" she asked.

"Why?"

She looked down at her brief attire, then back pointedly at Daniel. "Because I'm not exactly dressed for a motorcycle, that's why."

"So?"

She frowned at him. "What do you mean, 'So?' So I'm not going to be comfortable riding in this."

Instead of replying, he stood and placed his foot on the throttle, then shoved it down to bring the motorcycle roaring to life. "Look, I'm outta here. You can come with me or you can stay here with your girlfriends, but I've got better things to do than sit here waiting for you."

Olivia's first instinct was to tell him to shove off then, but something in his challenge riled her. Squaring her shoulders, she walked over to the back of the bike, glared at Daniel defiantly and hiked up a good bit of her little dress. She derived some satisfaction at the way his mouth dropped open at the ample view of her legs her action provided, and she lifted her finger beneath his chin to urge his mouth shut again. Then she hauled one leg over the seat of the big motorcycle, pulled herself deliberately as close to Daniel as she dared and held on tightly to his waist.

"What about helmets?" she asked as he straightened the bike and pushed back the kickstand.

"Helmets are for—" She lost his last word in the roar of the engine, but she was pretty sure it was something she'd be better off not hearing anyway.

"But isn't it illegal to ride a motorcycle without a helmet in New Jersey?"

"Yeah. So?"

"So we could get pulled over and ticketed."

"Don't worry your pretty little head about it, Livy. I'll handle the cops." He dropped a hand to her bare thigh and skimmed it backward until he reached the hem of her dress. "You just concentrate on handling me."

She rolled her eyes toward the sky. Oh, brother.

And with that, Daniel throttled the motorcycle forward, handling the big machine with as much prowess as he would if it were a part of him, as comfortable driving the bike as he was breathing. Olivia was amazed. Clearly, there was a lot about her neighbor she didn't know. A lot about him she wasn't sure she liked.

"Where are we going?" she asked over the rumble of the engine when they reached the end of their street and Daniel hung a left.

"A little place I used to frequent pretty regularly," he shouted over his shoulder. "The Dogbreath Saloon."

"The Dogbreath Saloon?" she echoed distastefully. "What's that?"

"A blast from the past," he told her as he moved them forward again. "A place where I can really be myself. Relax. You'll have a good time. Trust me."

Somehow, Olivia thought as she hugged herself closer to Daniel when their speed went way past the legal limit, the reassurance was anything but reassuring.

The Dogbreath Saloon was a typical Saturday night biker bar, not at all unlike the ones Olivia had frequented with Steve in her not-so-distant past. What little lighting permeated the smoke-filled room was dim and yellow, and the yeasty smell of years-old beer lingered like the heavily mascaraed barflies dotting the bar. The walls consisted of buckled plywood paneling interrupted occasionally by buzzing neon beer signs, and were decorated here and there with posters of big-breasted women in skimpy outfits who straddled outrageously large motorcycles.

A door in back led to a room furnished with a half-dozen pool tables, pinball machines pinging and video games boop-booping all around them. ZZ Top blared from a jukebox in the corner, and somehow Olivia was certain the beefy bartender popping the tab on a can of Schlitz behind the bar would be named something really colorful, like Snake or Meat or Deke.

"Morris," Daniel said to the man as he plopped himself down on a stool at one end of the bar.

Morris? Olivia repeated to herself as she took her seat beside him. The name seemed inappropriate for a man who had Death Before Minivans tattooed across his left forearm.

When the bartender looked up and saw Daniel, a wide, toothy smile replaced the scowl he had worn since their arrival. "Cobra!" he shouted out, reaching over the bar to clap Daniel hard on the shoulder. "Long time, no see, man. Where you been for the past couple years?"

Cobra? Olivia wondered. Who was Cobra? And why was this man acting like he knew Daniel extremely well?

"Yeah, it's been a long time," Daniel said, shaking the other man's hand. When he completed the action, he pulled a pack of cigarettes from his jacket pocket and lit one, smoking it as expertly as he had the previous one. "But I've been right here in Jersey. Bought a house in Collingswood."

Morris was clearly impressed. "Whoa, moving up in the world, aren't we? Well, you sure been absent from this place. What chased you off anyway? All those less-than-subtle hints from Wanda, I'll bet."

Daniel smiled, and Olivia was sure she was the only one in the bar who knew him well enough to see that he was blushing. "No, no, it wasn't Wanda. What happened there was a mutual parting of the ways. I've just been involved in other things, that's all."

"It's just as well," Morris said. "She's working for some cosmetics company now. Wears these pink business suits and comes into the bar sometimes with her sample case, wanting to do everyone's seasons for 'em. The place ain't been the same."

Without even asking what Daniel was drinking, Morris reached for a bottle of Blind Dog bourbon from the shelf behind him and poured a healthy shot into a glass. Then, with a flourish, he set it on the bar before Daniel. "And what'll you have, sweet thing?" he asked amiably when he turned to Olivia.

She smiled, hoping the gesture at least looked genuine. "Uh, whatever you have on tap is fine."

Morris obliged her, placing a frothy mug of beer in front of her before turning his attention back to Daniel again. "I just can't believe you're back after all this time. We all figured you got sent up to the pokey again for something."

"Sent up to the pokey *again?*" Olivia repeated, turning on her stool to face Daniel fully.

"Oh, sure," Morris said with a negligent wave of his hand. "Cobra here was a regular down at County." He smiled at Daniel. "Like that time you spent the weekend in the can for beating the hell out of that South Philly boy— remember that? What was that guy's name?"

"I don't remember," Daniel said, tossing back the bourbon in one swift gulp. He didn't even grimace when he completed the action.

"You beat somebody up?" Olivia asked incredulously. Daniel McGuane, the gentlest man she'd ever known, had beat the hell out of some nice boy from South Philly? Then the rest of Morris's announcement dawned on her. "You have an arrest record?" she asked, her voice fairly squeaking with her shock.

"Hey, the guy pulled a knife on Cobra," Morris said in Daniel's defense. Recollection dawned on him with the memory. "Yeah, that was the guy's name, too. Vinnie the Knife. He was a mean sonofabitch."

Olivia shook her head at Daniel. "You got into a knife fight with a guy named Vinnie the Knife?"

"Is there an echo in here?" Morris asked. "Hey, the guy was beating up his girlfriend at the time," he went on before Daniel could answer. "And we don't go for that kind of thing here at the Dogbreath. Cobra took him down a peg, let me tell you."

"I see," she said. Turning to Daniel, she asked, "And what are these other incidents for which you were a regular down at County?"

Morris was the one to reply again. "Fighting, mostly. Disturbing the peace. Cobra here always did have one short fuse, let me tell you. But he always had his reasons for his battles. 'Course, there were some incidents on his bike that got him in trouble, too. Refused to wear his helmet. And he took the cops on a merry chase more than once. But nothing too major."

"Mmm, hmm," Olivia murmured noncommittally.

"Except for that felony assault charge."

Olivia gaped at the bartender. "Felony assault?"

Morris nodded. "But that got thrown out. They could never prove Cobra was the guy they were looking for."

"And were you?" she asked Daniel.

He stared her square in the eye for the first time since he had arrived at her house that evening, and she wasn't sure she liked what she saw. "What do you think?" he asked quietly.

She shook her head. "Thanks to this conversation, I have no idea what to think about you anymore."

He smiled, an evil-looking curl to his lips unlike anything she'd ever witnessed from him before. "Good," he told her. "That's good."

When Olivia said nothing more, the big bartender turned back to Daniel. "Still got that Harley hog you were working on? The '67?"

Daniel shook his head, then nodded when Morris held up the bottle of bourbon to pour him another. "Naw, not that one. Sold it to a collector who was after me to buy it."

"Too bad. That thing was a beauty."

"Yeah, it was all right."

Olivia watched the byplay between the two men with much interest, all the while marveling at what she was discovering about her next-door neighbor. When Daniel tossed back the second shot without a flinch, she nearly choked on her sip of beer. She had never seen him consume anything alcoholic except for a very occasional glass of wine, and on those few occasions, he hadn't done it with nearly as much gusto. And *Cobra?* she wondered again. What was that all about?

"Hey, everybody!" Morris called out, drawing every eye in the bar to the couple. "Look who's here! It's Cobra!"

Delighted murmurings traveled through the room, and a large group of people suddenly appeared all around them, greeting Daniel by that odd nickname, slapping him on the back and shaking his hand. More than one of the women came forward to kiss him soundly on the lips, and Olivia felt herself go more rigid each time one of them did.

"Cobra?" she asked, bending toward his ear, keeping her voice low. "Knife fights? Felony assault? Harley hog? Blind Dog bourbon? Just what on earth is going on here, Daniel?"

He pointed toward his glass, and Morris filled it a third time. "You want a bad boy for a lover, Livy?" he asked without turning to look at her. "Well, you've come to the right place. Tonight you're going to learn something about me. And," he added as he lifted his glass to his lips, "with any luck at all, you'll learn a little something about yourself, too."

Before she could reply, a particularly buxom woman who was overly made-up, underdressed and hairstyled within an inch of her life, and who, to Olivia's way of thinking, was far too young to be hanging out in biker bars, sidled up to Daniel and draped an arm around his shoulder. "Who's your friend, Cobra?"

"Hi, Donna," he replied in a rough, throaty tone of voice Olivia had never heard him use before. "You've done a lot of growing up over the past couple years." He covered Donna's hand with his and lifted it to his lips, treating her palm to a loud kiss. Then, much to Olivia's surprise, he pulled the other woman into his lap. "My friend over there is named Olivia." Without looking at her, he added absently, "Olivia, this is Donna. Donna, Olivia."

"Hi," Donna said, also ignoring Olivia, focusing on the man into whose lap she had fallen instead.

Olivia narrowed her eyes and sipped her beer thoughtfully. "You know, Cobra," she said finally, moving to his other side so that he would be unable to avoid looking at her. She pointed to the young woman in his lap. "Fifteen will get you twenty. If you know what I mean."

"Oh, hey, Livy, Donna's all of twenty-one now, aren't you, kid?"

Donna corrected him. "Twenty-one and a half."

"I see," Olivia said. She moved back to Daniel's other side and rolled her eyes toward the ceiling. "Cobra," she muttered under her breath. "Sheesh."

She had intended her words to be too quiet for anyone else to hear, but she thought she noticed a small smile curl the edges of Daniel's lips. However, he continued to look at Donna—who continued to look back at him—obviously dismissing Olivia without a care. She let him get away with his disregard for a full two minutes before growing tired of it. If he had been doing something with Donna besides just staring at her—like talking, for example—she wouldn't have minded so much, but...

Oh, who was she kidding? she asked herself. As crazy as she knew the realization to be, she didn't want Daniel doing *anything* with another woman. Especially one who looked like Donna.

When she'd had enough, Olivia set her beer back on the bar and tapped Daniel pointedly on the shoulder. "Come on, Cobra," she said. "What say you and me take a little spin on the dance floor, hmm?"

He sighed dramatically and smiled at Donna. "Excuse me, will you?" he asked her. "Olivia wants to dance."

Donna frowned prettily, but acceded to his request. Olivia watched as she strolled down the bar to entwine herself with someone else, then turned to ask Daniel a few questions about his relationship with the young woman. But when she saw his face and noted the absolute warning etched there, she delayed voicing her curiosity.

Something was really wrong, she thought. Daniel wasn't at all like himself, and as the night had progressed, he had become more and more of a stranger to her. Tonight, he was dangerous somehow. Scary, even. And she didn't like the change in him for one minute.

"Don't ever tell me what to do again," he said, his voice low and level and completely menacing.

His vehemence surprised her. "What?" she asked. "What are you talking about? I wasn't telling you what to do. All I did was—"

"And don't contradict me," he warned her. Without further comment, he wrapped his fingers roughly around her upper arm and pulled her along behind him toward the dance floor.

"Ow, Daniel," she said, trying to wrench her arm free from his less-than-gentle grasp. "You're hurting me."

He ignored her objection and yanked her into his arms, dropping his hands familiarly to her backside to cup his hands firmly over her derriere.

"Daniel," she whispered, disconcerted by the intimacy of his posture. "This is a public place."

"So?"

She felt herself flush, and was uncertain whether the reaction was a result of embarrassment or anger. "So, I'm not comfortable being pawed like an animal."

When he didn't remove his hands as requested, but simply pulled her more fiercely against himself, she reached around behind herself and tried to move them for him, urging his hands up toward her waist. But the more she struggled with him, the more insistent his embrace became. When his fingers splayed open and journeyed down to the backs of her thighs to venture between her legs, Olivia gasped.

"Daniel," she said again. "Don't."

"Why not?"

"I told you why. I don't like being manhandled in public."

He ignored her request again, his smile growing salacious. "Oh, so you prefer to be manhandled in private?"

"No," she told him. "I prefer not to be manhandled at all."

He looked down at her thoughtfully. "That sure doesn't jibe with the kind of man you say you prefer. I would have thought that all those bad boys you claim to like would be pretty... shall we say *physical*... in their affections. And certainly more concerned with their own satisfaction than yours."

She tried not to squirm, tamping down her reluctance to agree with him. "Well, yeah, they are that... sort of. But—"

"But what?" he taunted. "You must like guys who are physical and careless, right? Why else would you waste your time on those bad boys unless you don't mind overlooking your own comfort in favor of their desires?"

"Actually, I *do* mind overlooking my own comfort for their..." She inhaled deeply, pushed away the confusion that Daniel was making her feel and tried again. "Look, that's not exactly what I meant when I said—"

"So, quit arguing with me and just enjoy yourself."

He pushed her toward him again, bringing her into much more meaningful contact with his lower extremities. A wild heat shot through her when she couldn't help but notice how aroused he was. Her eyelids fluttered closed, and any coherent thought she'd been about to voice completely fled her.

"Enjoy yourself," he repeated, his voice harsh and low. He dropped his head to the curve of warm skin that joined her shoulder to her neck, sucking a small portion of her flesh into his mouth before laving it with his tongue. "I know I'm enjoying myself."

"Oh, Daniel," she said with a groan, hating herself for letting him get to her this way. "Don't do that."

"But why not?" he murmured close to her ear. "You like it, I like it. What's the problem?"

She felt the tip of his tongue caress her lobe before moving upward to taste the inside shell of her ear. Her pulse rate quickened at the intimate touch, and she nearly forgot to be outraged by his blatant ignorance of propriety. "The problem is that we're surrounded by dozens of people," she whispered, feeling herself go weak in the knees.

"Oh, I can take care of that."

"You can?"

"Sure."

His voice had become a virtual purr, a mixture of passion and promise and something else Olivia wasn't quite able to identify. Something she wasn't sure she liked. Something that made her feel as if she'd be smart to put an end to the evening right now.

But when Daniel started dancing the two of them backward, rubbing his body sinuously against hers, dropping his head to nuzzle her neck and bite her gently again, all she could do was succumb to him. Because wherever Daniel was taking her, she found herself wanting to know more about their destination. She forgot about the swaggering arrogance he had affected that evening, forgot about how carelessly he had spoken to her, how easily he had ignored her requests. The damp heat of his breath on her neck and the circular motions of his hands on her thighs scrambled her thoughts completely. And all Olivia could do was let him have his way.

Eventually, she opened her eyes again and discovered that the two of them were indeed nearly alone. Daniel had danced her through the doorway to the game room where only a handful of patrons stood around one of the pool tables. With an expressive jerk of his head toward the door, the four men immediately cleared out, leering at Olivia on their way while clapping Daniel soundly on the back. The last one, she noted, tugged a curtain over the doorway behind him, and then she and Daniel were indeed alone in the room.

"Daniel, what—"

"Relax," he said again, interrupting her protest. He began the back-and-forth motions of their bodies again, swaying them slowly to and fro, completely out of time to the frenetic music audible from the other room.

"Don't tell me to relax," Olivia snapped, starting to feel frightened for no reason she could name. "I hate it when guys tell me to relax. It always means they're about to try something they have no business trying."

Daniel's normally affectionate smile was a leer. "And you love it when they do that, don't you?"

"No, like I just said, I *hate* it when they do that."

"Oh, you women may say you hate it, but you really love it."

She stared at him incredulously. "Excuse me? I'm sorry, Daniel, but I could have sworn I just heard you stupidly say that women really mean yes when they're saying no."

"Well, don't they?"

She curled her fingers into a fist and tapped lightly at his temple. "Hello? Is anyone in there? Anyone besides this big, thick-skulled Neanderthal who's posing as a human being?

What on earth is the matter with you tonight? You're acting like a jerk.''

"Nothing's the matter with me," he told her. "I'm just trying to be the kind of man you like."

"This is *not* the kind of man I like," she denied.

"Of course it is," he countered. "I've done everything you want a man to do. I've gone without shaving for a couple of days. I drove my motorcycle too fast and declined to wear my helmet. I drank my bourbon straight up. I'm ignoring conventional and societal mores. This is exactly what you described in your ideal man. I'm not stable, I'm not decent, I'm not good and I'm sure as hell not nice. I'm...dangerous. I'm everything you said you want in a man."

"That's not what I want in a man," she whispered.

But her voice carried none of the conviction she tried to feel. Because Daniel had just thrown her own words right back in her face. And deep down inside, she had to admit that—although pushing it to the extreme—he wasn't acting too entirely different from a lot of the guys she had dated in the past. But this was different. This was Daniel. He wasn't supposed to be like other guys. Because he *wasn't* other guys.

For the past few months, she'd seen more of Daniel McGuane than she had at all the other times in her life combined. She had sat with him on her back porch and talked to him while he was working, had shared breakfast, lunch and often dinner with him. She had shared her son with him. Had shared herself with him. And gradually, she had grown to like him more than ever. Eventually, she had come to see how good things could be between her and a man.

Olivia was tired of talking to Cobra. She was suddenly tired of all men who were rough and egocentric, who couldn't carry on a decent conversation with an intelligent woman. She opened her mouth to tell the overgrown baby just that when he pulled her close again.

"Isn't that exactly what you want in a man?" he asked.
"No."

"So you don't like it when a man does this?"

He dropped his hands to her waist again, strumming his fingers up over her rib cage as he plundered her mouth with his. When he reached her breasts, he curved his hands over them completely, stroking harder and more insistently before scooping aside completely the low-cut fabric and her lacy brassiere.

"Daniel, don't," she said, trying to brush his hand away so that she could cover herself again.

But he caught her hand in his and pushed it back down to her side, then lowered his head to nip at the tender flesh he had bared. An incandescent heat swept over her at the mixture of fear and passion that swept through her. Passion because it was Daniel who held her in his arms. Fear because the same man was also a stranger. And there was no way she would allow herself to be treated this way by a stranger.

"Stop it," she said, pulling herself free of him.

She backed away until one of the pool tables hindered her escape. Before she could dart to the side and through the curtain that offered her a dubious sanctuary, Daniel was upon her again, fastening a hand to the rim of the pool table on each side of her, pressing himself insistently against her.

"Come on, Livy," he murmured in a dangerously unconcerned voice. "Don't fight what you've been begging for all along."

She shook her head in silent denial, but couldn't find her voice to speak. From the other side of the curtain, she could hear the muffled strains of a raucous heavy metal tune. She felt the rim of the pool table pressing into her from behind, then gasped when Daniel settled his hands on her hips and lifted her up to sit on the worn green felt. Before she could voice her protest, he gripped her arms tightly and pushed her backward, until she was lying on her back in a position that was anything but comfortable and he was lying atop her.

This wasn't funny anymore. Until now, she had thought Daniel's performance a silly, ineffective charade. But what had begun as a pretense, something she was certain had been meant to teach her a lesson, had gotten far too out of hand. For the first time since she had met him, Olivia feared Daniel. Feared what he was threatening to do to her, what he suddenly seemed completely capable of carrying out. With a final, frantic push, she tried to heave him off of her, but to no avail. For one long, frightening moment, his gaze locked with hers. For one long, frightening moment, he was a complete stranger to her.

And then, as suddenly as his attack had begun, it ended. He levered himself up off her and stood at the foot of the pool table, then swiped a hand viciously across his face. His breathing came in ragged, rusty rasps, and his expression was grim.

"Is this the kind of man you want?" he spat at her, not even trying to hide his revulsion and resentment. "Is that the way you like it?"

She didn't respond, only scrambled into a kneeling position at the center of the table and covered as much of herself with her hands as she could.

"Because I hate it that way," he bit out. "I hate it. It's degrading and humiliating and has nothing to do with love."

When she was finally able to find her voice, Olivia said, "Why? Why did you do that?" She swallowed hard, struggling to catch her breath. "I don't understand what's come over you tonight," she went on in a hoarse whisper. "You're not yourself. Who's this guy, Cobra, you've been pretending to be?" She ran a shaky hand through her hair and tried to fight back the tears that filled her eyes. "Where's Daniel?" she whimpered, scooting to the other end of the pool table. "I want Daniel back."

"Oh, you've got Daniel right here, Livy. Daniel McGuane, the early version. This is the guy I used to be for a long, long time. Before I came to my senses. Before I realized what kind of man I was starting to become. This is the way I used to dress, the way I used to talk, the way I used to drink, to live, to act…. And this," he added, pointing to the pool table, "is the way I used to party. Granted, the women involved were generally more inclined to making love on a pool table than you are, but I had a point to make here tonight."

Olivia climbed down awkwardly and tried to stand, but found herself still clinging to the side of the table to keep herself from falling over. "That point being?" she asked.

"That eventually *I* came to my senses about living dangerously. I grew up, Livy," he said expressively. "It may have taken me over thirty years to do it, but *I grew up.*"

And with that, he turned away and marched steadfastly toward the door. As he tore aside the curtain to pass through it, he turned to look back at her one final time. His expression was pained and disappointed, though whether his reaction was a response to his own behavior or hers, Olivia wasn't sure. Then he exited the game room and left the curtain swishing silently behind him.

For a long time, Olivia only stood in place, watching the doorway, wondering if she had just dreamed everything that had happened. Then she looked down at the torn fabric of her dress, at the bruised flesh to the right of her breast and the bite mark on her shoulder. What had happened had been no dream. No dream, but certainly a nightmare.

At least Cobra was gone, she thought, sighing fretfully in relief. Hopefully for good. As she limped toward a pay phone on the other side of the room, she realized something else, as well. Daniel was also gone. And maybe he was gone for good, too.

Reaching into her pocket for the quarter Zoey had given her earlier, she pushed the thought away and plunked the coin into the slot. Zoey and Sylvie would really be curious now, she mused as she punched her home number. But Olivia didn't care about what her friends would think. She didn't care at all. The only thing she could think about now was Daniel, and wonder about his puzzling parting words.

Eleven

Olivia was up early the following morning. Mainly because she had slept little the night before. Not because Simon had been fussy—the baby was sleeping for longer and longer periods as he aged. And not because of Sylvie's incessant snoring—Olivia had gotten used to that when the two sisters were teenagers. The reason she had lain awake much of the night before was the same reason she had done so for many nights over the past few months. She had been completely preoccupied by thoughts of Daniel—and this time, Cobra—McGuane.

I grew up, Livy.... I grew up.

The words had circled and drummed in her brain for much of the night, penetrating deeper and deeper until they had almost become a litany. Was that what her problem was? she wondered. That she hadn't yet grown up? Daniel had called her immature that morning after the two of them had made love. But she was a thirty-two-year-old woman, an obstetrical nurse, a single mother. She'd been on her own for a decade and survived a wide range of life experience. She was in no way a child anymore.

Or was she?

She made her way downstairs to find Sylvie still sleeping soundly on the living room sofa, where she had collapsed around 3:00 a.m. during the last act of *Beefcake County Jail* and decided to stay until morning. Her blond, spiky hair was flat on one side, and her left hand covered half of her face. Olivia had thrown the afghan over her on her way up to bed, but Sylvie, ever the violent sleeper, had kicked it onto the floor and lay exposed to the cool morning in her T-shirt and panties.

Olivia shook her head. She pitied the man who ever wound up saddled with her sister. Sylvie was brash, blunt, completely unreserved about speaking her mind...and a very restless sleeper. But she was also very lovable in her own...unique...way, Olivia thought with a smile. Maybe the guy who snared her—if indeed a man existed who could hold his own with Sylvie Venner—would wind up with a prize instead of a liability after all was said and done.

"Sylvie?" she said quietly, dropping her hand to her sister's shoulder.

"Hmm?" Sylvie responded sleepily.

"Sylvie," Olivia repeated, shaking her shoulder gently. "Wake up."

Ever so slowly, Sylvie's eyes fluttered open and she managed to focus on the woman standing over her. "Livy?" she asked, squinting against the pale morning light. "What is it? What time is it?"

"It's about six-thirty," Olivia told her. "I just fed Simon and put him back down to sleep. Could you keep an ear open for him in case he wakes up again? I have to go out for a little while."

Sylvie pushed herself up into a sitting position and palmed her eyes. "At six-thirty in the morning?" She yawned widely and dropped a hand to scratch her ribs. "I can only hope you're headed down to Dougie's Donuts for a dozen jelly-filled. Although a few chocolate-covered would be nice, too. And maybe a couple glazed, now that I think about it." She yawned again, not bothering to cover her mouth. "Where else would you be going at this time on a Sunday morning?"

"I have to make a call on a neighbor."

Sylvie opened her eyes wider and stared at her sister dubiously. "Oh, that's going to win you friends in the neighborhood real quick. I know I love it when my neighbors want to come in and be entertained at some ungodly hour."

"I'm only going next door."

The other woman nodded her understanding. "Oh. Daniel. Or should I say Cobra?"

Over a bottle of Lambrusco and two boxes of microwave popcorn Olivia had told Sylvie and Zoey all that had transpired the night before. The other women had been as puzzled as she by Daniel's erratic conduct, but Zoey—who had minored in child psychology in college—had detected a pattern of childish, as opposed to childlike, behavior. Unfortunately, with her brain somewhat addled by the effects of the wine, she hadn't been able to quite remember what it had all meant.

Consequently, Olivia was no better off this morning than she had been the night before, and now the only way she was going to clear up this mess was by going to the source. And that meant seeing Daniel. As soon as possible.

"Just keep an ear tuned to Simon, okay?" she asked her sister.

Sylvie nodded. "No problem. Say, you do have some real coffee around here somewhere, don't you?"

"In the freezer. Next to the frozen waffles."

Sylvie smiled serenely. "Oh, Livy, you do know how to treat a guest like a queen."

"I won't be gone long."

"I bet you are," Sylvie said as her smile changed to speculative. She reached for the afghan on the floor and wrapped it around herself. "I bet you don't come back for hours."

Olivia considered her sister's challenge. "Will it...will it be a problem if I *am* gone for a little while? For, oh, I don't know, say an hour or so?" She lifted her shoulders in a negligent shrug. "Not that I'm expecting anything to happen, of course. Daniel and I just need to talk is all."

Sylvie's eyes fairly twinkled. "Of course," she agreed. "But no, it won't be a problem. Heck, stay gone all day if you want. Except that Simon might get hungry."

"There's some milk I expressed in the fridge," Olivia told her.

Sylvie smiled. "Then by all means, be gone all day if you want."

"Well, it won't be *all* day," Olivia said. "It's just in case...you know...in case we get started talking about something really serious that takes a little time, that's all."

"Talking," Sylvie repeated. "Mmm."

Olivia squeezed her sister's arm affectionately. "Thanks, Sylvie. I'll make it up to you someday when you're having man trouble."

"Man trouble?" she said. "Me? You've got to be kidding. There's not a man alive who could trouble me."

This time it was Olivia who smiled. "Oh, I bet there is somewhere. And I bet you meet him soon."

"Go away," Sylvie said, pushing at her sister's shoulder. "I have better things to do than sit around listening to you threaten me."

With a smile, Olivia did just that.

It wasn't until the fourth time Olivia rang the bell and pounded fiercely on Daniel's front door that she finally heard sounds coming from the other side. Slow sounds. Deliberate sounds. Sounds of shuffling feet and a body bumping into something that clattered loudly to the floor. That was followed by another curious sound, a sound she could have sworn was groaning.

Finally someone wrestled the door open from the other side, but the man who answered bore little resemblance to the man who had lived next door to Olivia for two years. Daniel's hair was limp and dull, scattered over his head as if horses had trampled it in his sleep. His face was sallow and seemed to be stretched taut over his skull, and his heavy beard of the night before was thicker and more ragged looking. His eyes were red rimmed and bleary, from what little she saw of them before he lifted a trembling hand to protect them from the glare of the rising sun.

Slumping forward, he leaned his other hand against the doorframe, making every effort to hold himself erect. Although he had managed to get his boots off and now stood barefoot, he had clearly slept in his clothes. He had also, she noted, dribbled what smelled like bourbon all over the front of his shirt.

"Daniel?" she asked experimentally by way of a greeting. "Or should I call you Cobra?"

He shook his head slowly, then winced at the pain. "No, it's definitely Daniel," he told her in a voice that reminded her of sandpaper rubbing over ice. "Cobra could handle his liquor. He never had a hangover like this in his life." He rubbed his eyes and squinted at her, looking not unlike Sylvie had a few moments before. "I knew I shouldn't have made Morris give me that bottle of Blind Dog to take home with me."

She grimaced in sympathy. "Did you finish the whole thing last night?"

He nodded, wincing again. "Most of it. I passed out somewhere along the way. Man, I never had this much trouble with bourbon before."

"Pity," Olivia said dryly with a rueful shake of her head.

"Yeah, it's amazing what a little clean living will do to thoroughly destroy what was once a perfectly good way to kill myself."

"Come on," she told him as she gently pried his white-knuckled grip off of the doorjamb and helped him back inside. "I'll fix you some breakfast. I need you to be coherent, because I have to talk to you."

"Livy?" he asked softly.

"Yes?"

"Would you please stop shouting at me?"

"I wasn't shouting," she said. "In fact, I was speaking more quietly than I usually do."

"Well, could you keep it down? You're going to make my brain explode."

"Some bad boy you turned out to be," she said softly, leading him back to his kitchen.

"I tried. I did my best to be bad. Honest."

"Well, thank goodness it wasn't enough."

She seated him in one of the fifties-styled plastic upholstered chairs at his fifties-style Formica-topped table and went to the refrigerator to scout around for suitable hangover fare. "Tomato juice," she announced triumphantly, pulling a can from the top shelf. "And celery. We can make you a nice virgin Mary. Too bad you don't have any bitters to go with."

"Top shelf over the stove," Daniel told her, dropping his head to cradle it carefully in his hands. "It's good in spaghetti."

"And you've got some real coffee," she added with delight as she inspected the contents of his freezer. "I knew you were a closet caffeine junkie."

"There are some mornings when a strict carbohydrate diet just doesn't cut it," he muttered.

With a more thorough search, Olivia located the fixings for pancakes, and although something really fatty like bacon and eggs would have been preferable, she whipped him up a fairly nice hangover reliever.

He looked infinitely better when he had scooped up the last of seven hotcakes with strawberry jam and downed the last of his third cup of coffee. But he still smelled like a distillery.

"Feel better?" she asked him.

He nodded, and she thought it a good sign that the gesture didn't seem to bother him at all. "Much better," he said, his voice having returned to the rumbling baritone she'd come to know and love.

"You'll feel even better after you have a shower," she told him.

He eyed her warily. "You trying to tell me something?"

"Mmm, hmm."

"What's that?"

"You stink."

He smiled, the first genuine smile she'd seen from Daniel in weeks. She smiled back.

"Well, hey, don't hide your feelings, Livy. If there's something you want to tell me, just come right out and say it."

"You need a shower," she told him. "I don't mind waiting."

"We need to talk," he corrected her. "And I *do* mind waiting."

"Okay," she agreed reluctantly. She wanted to talk, too. "Just stay downwind."

"No problem."

They sat in silence staring at each other for a long time, neither venturing to begin the conversation each knew was necessary. Olivia studied Daniel, noting with amazement how appealing he was, even looking the way he did. The light was back in his eyes, and except for his ragged clothes, gone was every trace of the man he had been the night before. The memory of last night made her recall that she had a question for which she desperately needed an answer.

"Daniel, what happened last night?" she asked him softly. "Why did you act the way you did? Why did you...why did you treat me like that?"

He lifted a hand to the back of his neck, rubbed hard and sighed. "Because I was tired of having you think I was Opie Taylor," he told her. "I was tired of you seeing me as some nice guy next-door neighbor who had nothing to offer you beyond a harmless little friendship. I had to show you that there was another side of me, however awful that side was. And I wanted you to see just how foolish you were to think that was the kind of man you wanted.''

"So you decided to play the part of some overbearing ape and treat me like I was a shank of beef to be devoured? That makes a lot of sense. That kind of behavior is certainly going to win me over to your way of thinking.''

"'That kind of behavior,' as you call it, was once perfectly normal for me.''

"I don't believe that for a minute.''

"Believe it. I was a real regular at the Dogbreath for a long time. And although those guys do have their good qualities, they're not exactly known for their concern over their health or their sensitive treatment of women. In short, they aren't very good influences. And like it or not, Livy, for a long time, I was one of them.''

"Then what turned you into the nice guy next-door neighbor?''

He frowned at her. "That's not all I am, you know.''

"Okay, okay. You're not Opie Taylor. But you are a decent guy, you can't deny that. So just how did Cobra become Daniel?''

He tipped his chair back on its hind legs, crossed his arms over his chest and stared at the ceiling. "It's not something I like to think about, you know? Not something I'm proud of. I've tried to put it all behind me, but I guess I'll never be able to escape completely from what I used to be, no matter how hard I try.''

Olivia bit her lip anxiously. This was clearly not something he wanted to tell her about, but she felt as though she had a right to know. If they had any hope of creating something meaningful together, then there couldn't be any secrets between them. She crossed her own arms over the table and leaned forward, silently indicating she had no intention of letting him off the hook. "So what happened?'' she asked.

"Until about two years ago, I had absolutely nothing going for me. I didn't have a steady job—just worked when I had to, when I needed money for gas or booze. My diet consisted of fast-food burritos and burgers, and I slept with any woman who took an interest, whether I liked her or not."

"Why?"

He shrugged. "Thinking back on it now, I have a vague idea. In the house where I grew up, self-respect was pretty substantially missing. My old man thought it was easier to silence a kid with a belt than to talk about what might be at the root of a problem. And my mother thought it wasn't a woman's place to question her husband. I guess I just never learned what it was like to feel good about myself, or to even care about myself. It never occurred to me that I might have some value, have something to offer."

Something twisted painfully inside Olivia at hearing his description of his home life as a child. Her own upbringing had been so loving, so rife with good feelings, she had never once thought there might be other kids in the world who had no idea what it meant to be truly happy. She hadn't begun to understand just how many unfortunate children there were until she got into nursing. "So what happened two years ago to change your mind?" she asked quietly.

He sighed, clearly unhappy to be recalling the memories in his head. "When I woke up one morning, there was an empty bottle of bourbon on the floor beside the bed, and a woman sleeping next to me I didn't recognize. I couldn't remember her name, where I'd met her, what the two of us had done or whether or not I had even taken any precautions to protect her or myself.

"Not that such a scenario was anything unusual," he added quickly, looking everywhere in the room except at Olivia. "But for some reason, that morning, it was like a little light went on in the back of my head. Between the booze, the smoking, the lousy diet, the motorcycle, the fighting, the sleeping around . . . I realized that what I was really doing was trying to commit suicide in some socially acceptable way. And I decided then and there that I was damned if I was going to let myself get away with it."

"Oh, Daniel..."

He held up a hand to stop whatever words of comfort or pity she had been about to offer. "Don't say anything. Like I said, it's a part of my life I'd just as soon forget about. That morning, I guess I realized my old man had done a number on me better than I thought he had. And I wasn't about to let that bastard turn me into what he had been. So I changed. Everything. Knocked off the liquor, the cigarettes, the bad eating habits, the sleeping around. I sold my motorcycle and moved out of my apartment and never went back to the Dogbreath again. Not until last night, anyway," he concluded with half a smile. When he finally turned to look at Olivia, his expression was concerned. "And you saw how that turned out."

"I can't imagine you as that man you were last night. It doesn't seem natural. It wasn't right." She paused for a moment before adding, "You scared me, you know."

He dropped his gaze to his lap before responding. "I know. And I'm really sorry about that. But I see a lot of what I was in you, Livy. Maybe you're not nearly as far-gone as I was two years ago, but there have been times when you've gotten yourself into a lot of trouble." He looked at her intently again. "And you're not the kind of person who just naturally attracts trouble. You go looking for it, whether you realize that or not. I needed to show you how dangerous that can be."

She nodded. "Sylvie says the same thing about me—that I'm self-destructive. So does Zoey. I guess I'm beginning to realize that you're all right. I don't know why, but I suppose I do create a lot of my own problems." She smiled, a wary, uncertain smile. "So, Daniel, tell me...what's it like being a grown-up? Is it scary?"

He arched his brows philosophically. "Actually, it's not as bad as you might think. I've been a grown-up for two years now, and I haven't buckled under the weight. Hey, I've worked steadily enough to earn a regular paycheck. I own a house. And I'm ready to take on even more responsibility. Hell, I'm even ready to—"

He stopped abruptly, something Olivia found puzzling. "What?" she asked. "You're even ready to what?"

He blushed, an action she was beginning to find endearing. "It's not important," he told her.

"I think it's very important," she countered. "What were you going to say?"

He sighed deeply and dropped his head to gaze down at the floor again. "A family," he said so quietly, she had to strain to hear him. "I'm ready to settle down and start a family."

Something deep inside Olivia, something warm and wild and wonderful, burst open in bloom at his roughly uttered declaration. "Don't you think it would help if you met the right woman first?" she asked, feeling breathless and excited for no reason she could name.

"Oh, I've met the right woman," he assured her, still looking down at the ground. "But she doesn't want a man like me."

"Maybe...maybe she'd like you better if you weren't so stinky," she said with a little laugh.

Daniel's head snapped up at that, his gaze fixing intently with hers. "What do you mean?"

"I mean a little shower can go a long, long way. Especially if you have someone there to scrub your back for you."

"Livy..."

"Come on. I'll talk to you while you clean up. Then afterward, we can talk some more."

"But, Livy..."

"Daniel, that bourbon smell is really beginning to make me woozy."

"But you'll talk to me while I shower?"

"Among other things," she said cryptically.

"Then what are we waiting for?"

* * *

"So, anyway, Zoey's such a big Ingmar Bergman fan, right? But you should have seen her watching *Beach Blanket Biceps,* Daniel. She was absolutely glued to the screen. Of course, she said she was only fascinated by the director's use of light and shadow, but Sylvie and I knew it was really Mr. October who had her going."

Daniel chuckled as he scraped the last of the stubble from his chin and ducked his face under the water rushing from the shower head. Olivia had been right about a shower making him feel even better. His hangover was well and truly gone. Now she sat on the other side of the shower curtain, doing her best to keep her chatter light and inconsequential, when deep down he knew they still had plenty to talk about that was anything but. He was just reaching for the shampoo bottle for a second sudsing when she started talking again.

"Yeah, Mr. October was all right, I guess, but he had nothing on other guys I've known."

Daniel stopped short of squeezing a handful of blue gel into his palm. "Other guys?" he asked.

"Sure," she replied breezily. He wished he could see her face.

"How many other guys?"

"Oh, at least ... one."

He was about to push the shower curtain aside to glare at her when he noticed a feminine hand grip it from the other side. Before he could utter even the slightest objection, Olivia's head poked around the curtain, too. "Yeah, Mr. October had nothing on you, Mr. McGuane," she told him after a frank appraisal.

"Livy!" he cried, dropping the tube of shampoo to grab for a towel. Awkwardly, he managed to wrap a substantial length of terry cloth precariously around his waist.

"So, you ready for me to scrub your back?" she asked. She looked down at the towel, now soaked from the shower stream, and grinned. "Oh, Daniel, come on. You don't need to be shy around me. We are friends after all, right?"

Her head disappeared then, and Daniel heard her moving around on the other side of the curtain. "Livy?" he called out warily.

"Very good friends," she continued as if she hadn't heard him. "In fact, you could say we're the best of friends."

"Uh, Livy?" he tried again.

"Hmm?"

"What are you doing out there?"

"I promised to scrub your back," she reminded him.

"So?"

The shower curtain opened once again, and this time Daniel saw all of Olivia standing there. Literally, *all* of Olivia, from her pink toenails to the soft flare of her naked hips to her rose-tipped breasts to the unruly mop of dark hair over merrily dancing brown eyes.

"So where do you want me to begin?" she asked, her voice low and throaty, sounding utterly aroused. She eyed him frankly. "Wow. The light's pretty good in here, isn't it?"

"Uh-huh," he mumbled, still staring at all the soft round places on her.

"Much better than it was the last time we—"

He dropped his towel and reached for her, lifting her over the side of the tub to haul her up against him. He swallowed her exclamation with a heartfelt kiss, rubbing his lips against hers as if he'd been starving for a taste of her. The hot water rushing from the shower sluiced over them, turning their bodies into slick, wet magnets, each drawing the other's touch as if dependent upon it for life.

Daniel felt Olivia's hands slide over him, starting at the base of his neck to dip lower, fingering every muscle on his back that tensed in response to her exploration. When she ventured lower, cupping her palms over his taut buttocks, he tore his mouth from hers, tilting his head back to groan in delight. He tangled his fingers in her wet hair and tipped her head backward, then bent over her to plunder her mouth again.

Deeper and deeper, he sought to possess her, and Olivia met every thrust with a demand of her own. He dropped his hands lower, to the sleek planes of her back and waist, pulling her closer, oblivious to the fact that they were virtually as close as two people could be. Pivoting their bodies to the left, he pressed Olivia up against the wet tile, then urged his body closer to her still.

She cried out at the exquisite feel of him against her, shuddered with ecstasy that a man so solid and strong could treat her with such care. This was Daniel, her Daniel, a man she had lost for a short time last night, but who had come back to her willingly, lovingly.

And suddenly it dawned on Olivia just what it was about Daniel that made him so different from other men. Suddenly she understood why he had left her feeling good when other men left her hurting. It wasn't because he was her friend, she thought. But precisely because he was her lover. Even before they had come together to satisfy a physical need, he had loved her. Somewhere deep inside herself, she had known that somehow, known it and responded to it.

And although it seemed so simple a revelation now, she hadn't realized until this moment that she had always loved him back. She didn't know how or why or when it had happened, but somewhere along the way, she had fallen in love with Daniel McGuane. That was why he had always been different. That was why she had always felt good with him.

"Oh, Daniel," she said, her voice soft and serene, completely at odds with the frantic feelings burning her up inside. "I love you. I love you so much."

He halted his onslaught enough to look at her, but continued to hold her close against him. "What?" he asked roughly, his voice scarcely above a whisper. "What did you say?"

She smiled, lifting her hands to frame his face. His wet hair hung over his forehead in straight points, his eyelashes spiked and looking thicker than usual. His eyes seemed bluer thanks to the reflection of the water and steam surrounding them, and tiny rivulets streamed down his cheeks, making her feel suddenly thirsty for something she'd never had before.

"I love you," she repeated, touching her lips to his for a brief, chaste kiss. "I think I've loved you since the day you moved in next door. I was just too stupid to realize it."

He stared at her for a long time as if afraid to believe what he'd just heard. Then slowly he began to smile, the expression completely altering his face. No longer did he look tired and anxious. With her one simple confession, she could see that she had made Daniel completely happy.

"I love you, too," he told her.

"I know."

"You do?"

She nodded. "I do now. And maybe I have all along—I don't know. But suddenly it's as if I can tell every little thing that's going on inside your head. It's almost as if I can read your mind."

His smile faltered a little. "Uh-oh."

"What do you mean, 'Uh-oh'?"

"If you can read my mind, then you must be picking up all the dirty thoughts I've been having lately."

She smiled. "Oh, you bet. And all I can say is that you're almost as creative as I am."

"Almost?"

"Almost. But that's okay. We have a long time to practice."

He bent to nibble her earlobe. "How long?"

She sighed, tightening her arms around his waist. "How long do you suppose it will take me to grow up?"

He lifted his hand and curved it over her breast, grinning when she moaned her pleasure. "From where I stand, Livy, you're a fully grown woman."

"That's good," she said with a sigh. "Because it's going to take two grown-ups to raise a baby."

He looked at her suspiciously, a little, she thought, hopefully. "What . . . what baby?"

"Our baby," she told him. "Simon."

He caught his breath, afraid to believe she meant what she was saying. "You . . . you consider Simon *our* baby?"

"Well, you said you'd be there for him if he ever needed you," she reminded him. "I'd say that makes you the best kind of father."

"Oh, Livy, nothing would make me happier than to claim you and that little baby as my own."

"Well, you've definitely got me," she said. "And I think Simon's going to be pretty keen on the idea, too."

"Marry me," Daniel said, kissing her fiercely again.

"Okay," she responded, kissing him back.

"How long before we can make another baby?"

"All the books say it would be best to wait two years."

"So we have two years to perfect our baby-making technique, is that it?"

"Yes."

"Then we better get started right away."

He reached for the faucet and shut the water off, then threw the shower curtain open wide. Olivia clung to him when he lifted her into his arms, and didn't let go until they were sprawled naked across his bed.

"We're going to get your sheets all wet," she murmured as he dipped his head to nuzzle the warm skin of her neck and shoulder.

"I'll say we are."

"Your bed won't be fit to sleep in."

"Sleeping isn't exactly what I have on my mind."

"You'll have to come over and stay with me and Simon for a while."

"Forever," he promised her.

"Forever," she agreed.

And then talking became difficult for Olivia, because Daniel dropped his head lower. He circled the peak of her breast with his tongue before moving lower still to taste her rib cage. She gasped when he dipped his tongue into her navel, and wound her fingers tightly into his hair when his journey continued south. Gently he tucked his hands beneath her hips and lifted her to kiss her more intimately than she had ever been kissed before. She groaned, gripping the sheets in her fists as she cried out his name and her love for him over and over and over.

And then she felt him move again, bringing his chest flush with her back, covering her belly with his splayed fingers. As he kissed the back of her neck, he pulled her leg over his thigh. And then she felt him inside her, moving deeper and deeper, touching her more thoroughly than she had ever been touched before.

"Daniel," she whispered, turning her face toward his. "Oh, Daniel."

He kissed her cheek and propelled himself more forcefully, faster and faster until she wasn't sure where he ended and she began.

"I love you," he whispered. "I love you."

And then she was lost to him completely. In a dizzying display of color and light, she was swept away into a maelstrom of delectation. She felt intoxicated, luxuriated, satiated. But most of all, she felt fulfilled. Sexually, emotionally, spiritually... in every way possible, Daniel McGuane had satisfied her, had made her feel complete.

"I love you, too, Daniel," she whispered as she slipped into a languid slumber. "I love you, too."

Epilogue

"**D**aniel, sweetheart, could you bring that extra pitcher of margaritas with you when you come out? And I'm ready for the hamburgers, too!"

"No problem, Livy!"

Daniel looked at six-month-old Simon and shook his head. "You hear the way your mother talks to me?" he asked the baby. "Like we're a couple of old married people." He lifted the baby from his high chair and kissed him loudly on the cheek, making his son giggle. "Isn't it great?"

Simon cooed and kissed him back. Well, what passed for a kiss anyway. Mostly Simon just leaned forward with his mouth open, leaving Daniel with an extremely wet cheek redolent of strained carrots. He hugged the baby tighter.

"You're a good guy, Simon," he whispered. "Just like your old man."

"Daniel?"

Olivia came into the kitchen from her backyard, wearing an oversize chef's hat, two oven mitts shaped like lobster claws and an apron that read *Who Invited All These Tacky People?* Her cheeks were pink from the brisk November air outside, and she was smiling. Autumn was well upon them, but they weren't going down without a fight. They had invited a few close friends to the house for one final barbecue, to say farewell to summer and to celebrate the quiet wedding at Olivia's house—now Olivia and Daniel's house—that had united them the week before.

"I've got the burgers ready," he told her, pointing at the cookie sheet full of perfectly formed patties on the table. "And the margaritas are coming right up."

"Great," she said. "But I also need to ask you about your house."

"My house?" he asked. "Which one? This one or the one next door?"

"Okay, your ex-house," she amended. "How long before it's finished? Zoey knows somebody who might be interested in renting it."

He shrugged. "I don't know. It probably won't be habitable before next summer."

"I'll tell her."

She turned to go, but not before Daniel caught her by the wrist. "Livy?"

She spun around again, her face a silent question mark.

"There's something I want to ask you."

"What?"

He paused for only a moment before stating, "I want to adopt Simon. I know you already consider us to be father and son," he added quickly, cutting her off before she could voice exactly what he knew she was thinking. "But I'd like to make it official. Legal. Like you and I have. I don't want to ever worry about losing him."

She smiled, her expression softening. "That's never going to happen."

"Nevertheless, I'd feel better if we had it in writing. You and I have made it official. Now I think the three of us should."

She smiled at him, her face a picture of love. "Okay. I don't think we'll have any trouble with Steve. And I even know where to find him. I ran into a mutual friend of ours a couple of weeks ago who knows where he's living now. It shouldn't be a problem."

He sighed, releasing a breath he hadn't been aware of holding. "Great."

Instead of turning to go back outside, Olivia removed her lobster claws and came to Daniel and their son, circling the bigger man's waist with one arm while lifting a hand to the baby's cheek.

"I never knew it could be this good," she said, tucking her head under Daniel's chin.

He held her close. "Neither did I."

"I've got it all. A friend, a lover, a family... What more is there, you know?"

"What indeed?"

"Of course, it would be nice if I could drop a couple more dress sizes."

Daniel chuckled. "There's nothing wrong with being a cozy size six, Livy. Besides, I like a woman with a little meat on her bones. You fill out a dress better than anyone I know."

"Well, that's true," she agreed, all modesty aside.

Simon slapped a wet palm against each of their faces and laughed. "Dada," he said, smiling at Daniel.

Daniel and Olivia, thoroughly astonished, dropped their mouths open in unison, looked first at each other, then at the baby, then laughed in amazement.

"What did you say, sweetie?" she asked the baby.

But Simon only smiled and refused to repeat his comment.

"Come on," Daniel cajoled. "Say it again. Say 'dada,' Simon. Come on. Say 'dada.'"

"No, say 'mama,'" Olivia countered. "Say 'mama' first."

Simon's gaze traveled from his father to his mother and back again. He squealed, widening his eyes at the sound, then reached for Daniel's nose and squeezed it hard.

"Dada," he said again.

Olivia laughed, hugging both men close. "'Dada,'" she repeated. "That's exactly what you are, Daniel McGuane. Ever since the day he was born, I've wanted Simon to have a dad like you." Her eyes filled with tears as she leaned over to kiss him hard on the mouth. "Who could have guessed he and I would be so lucky, so blessed, to wind up with the real thing?"

Daniel hugged his family to his heart and couldn't say a word. Olivia and Simon weren't the only ones blessed by fortune, he thought. He just wished everyone could be as happy as he.

* * * * *

Get Ready to be Swept Away by
Silhouette's Spring Collection

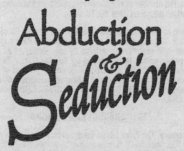

Abduction & Seduction

These passion-filled stories explore both the dangerous
desires of men and the seductive powers of women.
Written by three of our most celebrated authors, they are
sure to capture your hearts.

Diana Palmer
Brings us a spin-off of her Long, Tall Texans series

Joan Johnston
Crafts a beguiling Western romance

Rebecca Brandewyne
New York Times bestselling author
makes a smashing contemporary debut

Available in March at your favorite retail outlet.

MILLION DOLLAR SWEEPSTAKES (III)

No purchase necessary. To enter, follow the directions published. Method of entry may vary. For eligibility, entries must be received no later than March 31, 1996. No liability is assumed for printing errors, lost, late or misdirected entries. Odds of winning are determined by the number of eligible entries distributed and received. Prizewinners will be determined no later than June 30, 1996.

Sweepstakes open to residents of the U.S. (except Puerto Rico), Canada, Europe and Taiwan who are 18 years of age or older. All applicable laws and regulations apply. Sweepstakes offer void wherever prohibited by law. Values of all prizes are in U.S. currency. This sweepstakes is presented by Torstar Corp., its subsidiaries and affiliates, in conjunction with book, merchandise and/or product offerings. For a copy of the Official Rules send a self-addressed, stamped envelope (WA residents need not affix return postage) to: MILLION DOLLAR SWEEPSTAKES (III) Rules, P.O. Box 4573, Blair, NE 68009, USA.

EXTRA BONUS PRIZE DRAWING

No purchase necessary. The Extra Bonus Prize will be awarded in a random drawing to be conducted no later than 5/30/96 from among all entries received. To qualify, entries must be received by 3/31/96 and comply with published directions. Drawing open to residents of the U.S. (except Puerto Rico), Canada, Europe and Taiwan who are 18 years of age or older. All applicable laws and regulations apply; offer void wherever prohibited by law. Odds of winning are dependent upon number of eligibile entries received. Prize is valued in U.S. currency. The offer is presented by Torstar Corp., its subsidiaries and affiliates in conjunction with book, merchandise and/or product offering. For a copy of the Official Rules governing this sweepstakes, send a self-addressed, stamped envelope (WA residents need not affix return postage) to: Extra Bonus Prize Drawing Rules, P.O. Box 4590, Blair, NE 68009, USA.

SWP-S295

SILHOUETTE®

Desire®

is

DIANA PALMER'S
THAT BURKE MAN

He's rugged, lean and determined. He's a Long, Tall Texan. His name is Burke, and he's March's *Man of the Month*—Silhouette Desire's 75th!

Meet this sexy cowboy in Diana Palmer's THAT BURKE MAN, available in March 1995!

*Man of the Month...*only from Silhouette Desire!

DP75MOM

Robert...Luke...Noah
Three proud, strong brothers who live—and love—by

THE CODE OF THE WEST

Meet the Tanner man, starting with Silhouette Desire's *Man of the Month* for February, Robert Tanner, in Anne McAllister's

COWBOYS DON'T CRY

Robert Tanner never let any woman get close to him—especially not Maggie MacLeod. But the tempting new owner of his ranch was determined to get past the well-built defenses around his heart....

And be sure to watch for brothers Luke and Noah, in their own stories, COWBOYS DON'T QUIT and COWBOYS DON'T STAY, throughout 1995!

Only from

SILHOUETTE... **Where Passion Lives**

Don't miss these Silhouette favorites by some of our most
distinguished authors! And now you can receive a discount by
ordering two or more titles!

SD#05786	QUICKSAND by Jennifer Greene	$2.89	☐
SD#05795	DEREK by Leslie Guccione	$2.99	☐
SD#05818	NOT JUST ANOTHER PERFECT WIFE		
	by Robin Elliott	$2.99	☐
IM#07505	HELL ON WHEELS by Naomi Horton	$3.50	☐
IM#07514	FIRE ON THE MOUNTAIN		
	by Marion Smith Collins	$3.50	☐
IM#07559	KEEPER by Patricia Gardner Evans	$3.50	☐
SSE#09879	LOVING AND GIVING by Gina Ferris	$3.50	☐
SSE#09892	BABY IN THE MIDDLE	$3.50 U.S.	☐
	by Marie Ferrarella	$3.99 CAN.	☐
SSE#09902	SEDUCED BY INNOCENCE	$3.50 U.S.	☐
	by Lucy Gordon	$3.99 CAN.	☐
SR#08952	INSTANT FATHER by Lucy Gordon	$2.75	☐
SR#08984	AUNT CONNIE'S WEDDING		
	by Marie Ferrarella	$2.75	☐
SR#08990	JILTED by Joleen Daniels	$2.75	☐

(limited quantities available on certain titles)

AMOUNT	$_____
DEDUCT: 10% DISCOUNT FOR 2+ BOOKS	$_____
POSTAGE & HANDLING	$_____
($1.00 for one book, 50¢ for each additional)	
APPLICABLE TAXES*	$_____
TOTAL PAYABLE	$_____
(check or money order—please do not send cash)	

To order, complete this form and send it, along with a check or money order
for the total above, payable to Silhouette Books, to: **In the U.S.:** 3010 Walden
Avenue, P.O. Box 9077, Buffalo, NY 14269-9077; **In Canada:** P.O. Box 636,
Fort Erie, Ontario, L2A 5X3.

Name:_____

Address: _____ City:_____

State/Prov.:_____ Zip/Postal Code:_____

*New York residents remit applicable sales taxes.
Canadian residents remit applicable GST and provincial taxes. SBACK-DF

Silhouette®